The Image Of Her Son Placing His Small Hand In Nick's Would Be Burned In Her Memory Forever.

At that moment, Maggie felt as if time had stopped, as if the world had stopped and nothing else existed but the two of them. The two men in her life who had changed her the most, both of them unintentionally altering her life forever. And neither one of them had a clue how important they were to her.

She found a calm in that moment. There'd been no reason for her to be so afraid of them meeting.

In a hundred years, Nick Santos would have no reason to believe that Drew was his son.

How could he, when Nick himself didn't even realize that he'd made love to her?

Dear Reader,

Silhouette Desire matches August's steamy heat with six new powerful, passionate and provocative romances.

Popular Elizabeth Bevarly offers *That Boss of Mine* as August's MAN OF THE MONTH. In this irresistible romantic comedy, a CEO falls for his less-than-perfect secretary.

And Silhouette Desire proudly presents a compelling new series, TEXAS CATTLEMAN'S CLUB. The members of this exclusive club are some of the Lone Star State's sexiest, most powerful men, who go on a mission to rescue a princess and find true love! Bestselling author Dixie Browning launches the series with *Texas Millionaire*, in which a fresh-faced country beauty is wooed by an older man.

Cait London's miniseries THE BLAYLOCKS continues with *Rio: Man of Destiny*, in which the hero's love leads the heroine to the truth of her family secrets. The BACHELOR BATTALION miniseries by Maureen Child marches on with *Mom in Waiting*. An amnesiac woman must rediscover her husband in *Lost and Found Bride* by Modean Moon. And Barbara McCauley's SECRETS! miniseries offers another scandalous tale with *Secret Baby Santos*.

August also marks the debut of Silhouette's original continuity THE FORTUNES OF TEXAS with Maggie Shayne's *Million Dollar Marriage*, available now at your local retail outlet.

So indulge yourself this month with some poolside reading— the first of THE FORTUNES OF TEXAS, and all six Silhouette Desire titles!

Enjoy!

Joan Marlow Golan
Senior Editor

Please address questions and book requests to:
Silhouette Reader Service
U.S.: 3010 Walden Ave., P.O. Box 1325, Buffalo, NY 14269
Canadian: P.O. Box 609, Fort Erie, Ont. L2A 5X3

SECRET BABY SANTOS
BARBARA McCAULEY

SILHOUETTE *Desire*®
Published by Silhouette Books
America's Publisher of Contemporary Romance

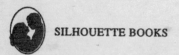

SILHOUETTE BOOKS

ISBN 0-373-76236-4

SECRET BABY SANTOS

Visit us at www.romance.net

Printed in U.S.A.

BARBARA McCAULEY

was born and raised in California and has spent a good portion of her life exploring the mountains, beaches and deserts so abundant there. The youngest of five children, she grew up in a small house, and her only chance for a moment alone was to sneak into the backyard with a book and quietly hide away.

With two children of her own now and a busy household, she still finds herself slipping away to enjoy a good novel. A daydreamer and incurable romantic, she says writing has fulfilled her most incredible dream of all—breathing life into the people in her mind and making them real. She has one loud and demanding Amazon parrot named Fred and a German shepherd named Max. When she can manage the time, she loves to sink her hands into fresh-turned soil and make things grow.

To Barbara Ankrum,
whom I alternately curse and bless for
making me work so hard.
Thanks, Babs.

One

Nick Santos was the boy whom mothers in Wolf River, Texas, warned their daughters about. His smile alone could charm fire from the devil, but his eyes, Lord Almighty, those eyes. Dark, mysterious eyes that all but consumed. Stay away from the likes of *that* boy, mothers would say with a shake of a finger. Nick Santos was trouble with a capital *T*.

He was fast, he was bad, and after twelve long, lucrative years on the motorcycle racing circuit, he was back.

No one was more surprised than Nick at his return. He thought he'd only come back to Wolf River to see his best friend, Lucas Blackhawk, get married. There certainly hadn't been any plans to stick around. Nick Santos never stuck around. Never called any place home.

But now Nick realized that even before he'd returned

to Wolf River to be Lucas's best man, something had been quietly prodding him back here. Nothing he could name, just some invisible nudge, some unexplainable force that wouldn't let him be. He'd figured that once he came back, the feeling would pass faster than a Ferrari around a ten-wheeler on the open highway.

That was six months ago. He'd not only stuck around, but at the ripe old age of thirty-three, he'd quit the racing circuit and opened up his own business: Santos Custom Cycles. Not for money—he had more of that than he knew what to do with. He didn't give two whits about the bottom line on his earnings statement. He simply enjoyed making things work, taking them apart, putting them back together again better than before. Machines fascinated him, and his ability to master them gave him a rush that racing once had before he'd burned out.

He might not race anymore, but he still had a way with motorcycles that bordered on the supernatural. There was nothing that Nick couldn't make a bike do. He had "the touch," as the old-timers would say with reverence.

Of course, women said that about Nick, too.

With reverence.

He'd had little time for female companionship these past six months. His business had taken off the minute word had gotten out to the motorcycle community that four-time National Championship winner Nick Santos had opened up his own shop. Customers were lining up from all across the country to have Nick customize a bike for them. He barely had time to ride himself, let alone free time for…extracurricular activities.

Standing in front of the frozen food section at Bud and Joe's Market, Nick sighed at the pathetic state of his romantic life. He considered the invitation for dinner that Sue Ann Finley had extended a few hours ago: red wine, juicy steak, Texas-size baked potato. And dessert, she'd murmured with a throaty whisper, was a surprise. As if he couldn't guess. He thought about the attractive brunette's lush body, her big brown eyes. On a whimper, he opened the freezer door and let the blast of cold slither through his jeans and flannel shirt.

But tempting as Sue Ann's offer was, he had a carburetor to rebuild and four cylinders to bore by nine o'clock tonight if he didn't want to deal with a screaming customer tomorrow. He hadn't been able to face one more takeout hamburger or pizza, so he'd decided that a frozen dinner was as close to a home-cooked meal as he was going to get.

And what choices he had. He frowned at the freezer case. Manly Man's Fried Chicken and Mashed Potatoes. Gideon's Gourmet Cheesy Chicken Pot Pie. Chef Richard's Macho Macaroni and Cheese. Frozen was quick and easy, and within his limited realm of cooking abilities, but it was also a far cry from that juicy steak and big steaming baked potato he'd been fantasizing about.

And speaking of fantasies...

He only caught a glimpse of hair the color of fall leaves as she turned the corner, but it was enough to tempt him away from the freezer aisle for a quick peek. He snatched a bag of chocolate chip cookies from the end display, then sauntered casually around the corner.

He'd been right about the hair. Deep red, it glittered with browns and golds and tumbled loosely around the shoulders of her cream silk blouse. Her waist would fit a man's hands perfectly, but then, so would her slender hips and rounded bottom. The snug coffee-brown slacks she wore more than suggested long, curvy legs.

She stood no more than four feet away, in front of a six-foot-tall, circular display of canned green beans, a bright blue hand basket in the crook of her arm, her back to him as she studied a list in her hands.

Who was she? he wondered, moving closer as he feigned interest in a shelf of dried fruit. She couldn't live in Wolf River, he definitely would have spotted this woman before if she did.

He grabbed a bag of dried noodles from the end of the shelf so he could move closer, and that's when he caught her scent. Feminine. Seductive. Incredibly enticing. He reached for a bag of elbow macaroni and inched closer still.

Turn around, he prayed silently, anxious to see if the face matched the body.

And then she did turn around.

He forgot to breathe as he stared at her. The heart-shaped face absolutely went with the body. Porcelain skin, upturned rosy lips, large expressive moss-green eyes that slowly lifted and looked at him.

When their eyes met, she went still. Her skin paled as she stared back.

She recognizes me, he thought with smug confidence, then flashed the smile that had graced more than a few celebrity sports pages and conquered even the most resistant female.

"Hi," he said with smooth charm. She seemed immobilized, and he took that as a positive sign. "I'm Nick Santos."

Her eyes widened at his introduction, then her lips moved, but no sound came out. Without warning, she whirled and ran smack dab into the tower of green beans.

The tower crumbled with a loud clatter. The woman went down with it; cans spilled over her, then rolled across the aisle in every direction.

Geez, he'd had all kinds of reactions from women, but never one quite like this.

Dismayed, Nick set his groceries down and knelt beside her. "Are you all right?"

She nodded, but refused to look at him, just waved him off. When he took hold of her shoulders to pull her up, she jumped in his hands as if he'd burned her.

"Maggie! Are you all right?"

George Kromby, the store manager and former high school classmate of Nick's, came running down the aisle, his white apron flapping like wings around his short, round body.

She glanced up sharply, and the look on her flushed face, one of utter despair and complete terror, baffled Nick. Certainly she wasn't afraid of him, was she? He didn't even know the woman.

Or did he?

Maggie...Maggie...

There suddenly seemed something vaguely familiar about her, though he couldn't pinpoint what it was. The scent of her perfume and the feel of warm silk under his hands was making it difficult to concentrate.

"Maggie, are you hurt?" George knelt beside them.

"Fine. I'm fine." Her words were strained, but there was a soft, husky tone to her voice that seeped into his already heated blood. He realized that he didn't want to let her go, but she twisted away from him and stood on her own. "I'm sorry, George. I wasn't watching where I was going."

"I told Rickie that display was too high." George fussed over her, gathering up her purse and basket as he criticized the clerk who'd built the skyscraper of green beans. Nick realized that the manager was just as captivated with the redhead as he was. Nick frowned at George, sending mental warnings that he'd seen her first.

"It was my fault completely. Please forgive my clumsiness." Maggie smoothed the front of her slacks, then flashed George a smile that made him blush to the roots of his thinning brown hair. "I'm sorry, but I've got to get home."

Without so much as a glance at Nick, she turned and disappeared down the soup aisle.

"Tell Mrs. Smith I said hello," George called after her.

Mrs. Smith?

Maggie Smith?

That woman, Maggie, was skinny little Margaret Smith, with the ragtop red hair and big glasses?

The last time he'd seen her was twelve years ago, just before he'd left Wolf River. He'd been working at the machine shop, and she'd come in with her father who'd needed the pistons of his 1956 Chevy bored. Nick had been twenty-one at the time, so she must have been about sixteen or seventeen. Margaret was the shyest girl he'd ever met. He'd always said hello to her, and she'd always mumbled a hello back, but never once did she actually look at him.

Obviously she was as shy now as she'd been growing up. She *still* wouldn't look at him, he thought to his annoyance, but he'd certainly looked at her. He just couldn't believe what he'd seen. Little Margaret Smith, with a killer body and gorgeous face. If that didn't beat all.

Her perfume lingered in the air, and it suddenly dawned on Nick that both he and George were still staring in the direction of the aisle she'd vanished down.

Nick gave the other man a friendly slap on the back. "Hey, George, let me give you a hand here with these cans."

"What?" George blinked, then looked at Nick. "Oh, ah, that's all right, Nick. I'll take care of it."

"No problem." Nick bent and reached for a can. "So, how are Mr. and Mrs. Smith?" he asked casually. "They still living over on Belview Avenue?"

Nodding, George scooped up several cans and began to stack them. "Mr. Smith went in for knee surgery last week. Maggie flew in from New York yesterday to give her mom a hand."

So that's why he hadn't seen her before, Nick realized. She'd just got into town. Bad for Mr. Smith's knee, but good for him, Nick thought. "New York, huh? She work there?"

"Mrs. Smith says she's a journalist with some big newspaper." George took pride in his job and meticulously straightened the cans to line up the labels. "Has her own column and everything."

Nick spotted a credit card lying under a pile of cans and picked it up. "Margaret Hamilton." Damn. She was married. "That must be her husband I saw waiting out front. Big guy with blond hair?"

"Maggie's divorced." George glanced over his shoulder and frowned. "You fishin', Nick?"

Nick resisted the urge to grin at the good news, then slipped the credit card in his shirt pocket. "Nah, not me, pal. Too busy for females right now." Nick winked at George. "But you know how that is."

"Yeah, right." George rolled his puppy-dog eyes. "Just last night I had to tell Cindy Crawford I'd have to get back to her."

"Iris Sweeney will be disappointed to hear that," Nick said, deciding that a little matchmaking for George would not only boost the man's ego, but keep him from looking in other directions.

"Iris Sweeney?"

Nick nodded. "Just last week I heard her say you have the best-looking produce section she's ever seen."

"No kidding?" George said with a quick grin, then cleared his throat and gave a reserved shrug of his shoulders. "I am rather proud of the organic vegetable display."

"As you should be." Nick hadn't seen a vegetable in weeks. Unless you counted tomatoes on pizza or lettuce on hamburgers. He doubted they were organic, though. On an impulse he snatched up two cans of green beans. "Gotta run, George. See you around."

"Try a can of mushroom soup and cheese with those beans," George called after him. "They make a great casserole."

Five minutes later, his shopping done, carburetor and pistons forgotten, Nick roared out of Bud and Joe's parking lot and headed for Belview Avenue.

Nick Santos was back.

Still in a daze, Maggie had driven back to her parents' house and squeezed her compact rental into the garage beside her father's yacht-size 1977 Buick. The radio blasted a loud, heavy-metal song that she never would have listened to under ordinary circumstances, but she'd been too shaken to even notice the ear-piercing noise. She shut off the engine, but a loud roar still pounded in her head.

Nick Santos was back.

She wouldn't have believed it, except for the fact that he'd spoken to her and touched her. *My God,* she closed her eyes and drew in a deep breath. He'd actually touched her.

She was still too much in shock to even be embarrassed that she'd dived head first into a display of green beans and landed on her bottom. So much for conquering her childhood awkwardness, she thought dismally. So much for her five years as a confident, assertive journalist. One look at Nick Santos and it all went out the window.

If there was one person Maggie never expected to see again—one person she never *wanted* to see again—it was Nick Santos.

What was he doing here? She pressed her forehead to the steering wheel and let the wave of panic wash over her. Nick had left Wolf River twelve years ago, two years before she'd gone off to Boston for college. He'd become an overnight success with his racing. The media loved him, not only for his good looks and charm, but for his involvement with charities. She even remembered that several years ago he'd done a magazine spread for a blue jeans company and donated his endorsement to a children's charity.

Nick Santos, with his heart-stopping smile and his take-your-breath-away eyes. He'd been in countless magazine articles, photographed at celebrity parties, hounded by the tabloids in search of dirt outside the motorcycle racing track.

But there was one article she remembered above all the rest. The paternity suit he'd been involved in five years ago. There'd been pictures of him beside a beautiful blonde and a caption that read: Santos Soon to Be a Daddy? The Courts Will Decide.

He'd eventually won that case, his lawyer proving that the woman had lied and was simply looking for some easy money. But the battle had been nasty, as well as highly publicized, and no stone in Nick's life had been left unturned: his alcoholic mother who'd abandoned him when he was ten, an abusive stepfather, his year at Wolf River's County Home for Boys when he was fourteen, and his close, lifelong friendship with Lucas Blackhawk and Killian Shawnessy. Nick's life had been an open book to the world.

And still he'd smiled through it all, refusing to talk about his past or the court case with reporters, but dazzling them nonetheless with his wit and charm. He was smooth, but rough enough around the edges to make women sigh with pleasure and men grunt with approval.

And he was back. God help her, he was back.

She drew in another long, slow breath and stepped out of the car. Her knees still felt shaky, but she was determined not to let her parents see that anything was wrong. When she let herself in the front door, the smell of roast beef filled the house. If there was one thing her mother loved to do besides talk it was cook.

"Margaret, you're back so soon." Her mother came out of the kitchen, wiping her hands on a dishrag. In spite of her compulsive need to feed everybody who entered the house, Angela Smith was trim herself, a pretty brunette with warm brown eyes and a flashing smile. "Did you find everything all right? That new stock boy George hired has moved everything around so that my head spins just looking for a loaf of bread. Last week it took me ten minutes to find the prune juice. Which reminds me—'' she turned toward the living room ''—Boyd, have you had your glass today?''

Maggie's father grunted from behind the newspaper he was reading. Bandages circled the knee of one swollen white leg, which he'd propped up on the ottoman of his easy chair, but his blue-plaid bathrobe sufficiently covered the rest of him.

Maggie realized she hadn't bought one thing. How could she have gone grocery shopping after seeing Nick? "I...lost the list you gave me. I'll have to go back."

"Never you mind, honey. There's nothing that won't keep till tomorrow. Dinner's almost ready." Her mother frowned. "You look a little pale, dear. Is anything wrong?"

"No, nothing. Of course not. I'm fine, just fine."

Not wanting her mother to see the lie, Maggie turned away quickly and set her purse on the entry table. Angela Smith knew everything that went on in Wolf River. Hadn't her mother told her, in detail, about Helen Burnette's divorce? About Susan Meyers's argument with Phyllis White over her poodle's constant barking? About Ralph Hennesy's fender bender with Walt Johnson?

How could she tell her all those things and never once mention that Nick Santos was living here again? The man was a celebrity, for God's sake.

Maybe Nick wasn't really living here, Maggie reasoned. Maybe he was just visiting Lucas Blackhawk. Maggie knew that Lucas had married Julianna Hadley a few months back and that Nick had been the best man. Her parents had been invited to the wedding reception, almost everyone in town had been. Her mother had talked endlessly about Lucas and Julianna and what a wonderful couple they made. But when she'd made a fuss over how handsome Nick had looked in his suit, how charming he'd been when he'd asked her to dance, Maggie had quickly made an excuse and hung up the phone. She couldn't talk to her mother about Nick. She couldn't.

She couldn't talk to anyone about Nick. Ever.

"Sweetheart, are you sure you're all right?"

Maggie realized that she'd been staring blankly into the mirror over the entry table, and that her mother was watching her now, her eyes narrowed with concern.

"Just a little jet lag, Mom." She turned and gave her mother a hug. "I'll go check on Drew, then put the potatoes on."

"Drew hasn't budged from the video you put on before you left, and the potatoes are already boiling. Oh, and that reminds me. Miss Perry, the preschool director from the elementary school called. They have an opening if you'd like to take Drew in on Monday."

Thank goodness for that, Maggie thought. A four-year-old with too much time on his hands was like a tornado waiting to touch down. He'd be much happier playing with other children, and she'd be more sane. At least, she'd thought she would be, until she'd run into Nick. Keeping her sanity now was going to be much more difficult.

"You go rest up." Her mother was already scooting her toward her old bedroom. "I'll call you when dinner is ready."

Maybe she would rest a little, Maggie thought. A

few minutes alone would give her enough time to pull herself together again. Seeing Nick had been a fluke, an unfortunate coincidence. He was probably just passing through town and stopped to say hello to Lucas. And even if he did stick around for a few days, Wolf River wasn't all *that* small. The odds of running into him again were practically non-existent.

That thought eased the tightness in her shoulders. She could only imagine what he must think of her after her insane behavior in the market. No doubt he thought she was a crazy lady escaped from the funny farm.

Fine. Let him think she was crazy. As long as she didn't have to see him again, he could think whatever he wanted.

On her way to the bedroom, Maggie leaned over and brushed her father's whisker-rough cheek with her lips. He'd retired only six months ago from his foreman construction job and he'd had way too much time on his hands. Even after thirty-six years of marriage, her mother, who had the patience of a saint, was ready to murder the man. And if he'd been a pain-in-the-behind before, since his surgery, he'd been twice as gruff. As far as patients went, he was somewhere between Oscar the Grouch and Attila the Hun. "Can I get you anything, Daddy?"

"Sneak me a shot of whisky and a cigar," he said in his deep gravelly voice without looking up from his paper. "There's cash in it for you."

"Money won't do me any good if I'm dead. Mom says no alcohol or tobacco while you're recuperating, and if she so much as catches a whiff of either on your breath, she'll bruise both our behinds."

His response was something between a growl and a grunt. He simply snapped his paper and mumbled something about overbearing wives and ungrateful children.

At the sound of the doorbell, she straightened.

"Would you get that for me, Maggie?" her mother called from the kitchen. "Jim Becker's stopping by with a set of crutches for your father. He's supposed to be up walking by the end of the week."

Maggie smiled when her father only buried his head deeper into his paper. Getting a six-foot, two-hundred-pound, stubborn man walking was no stroll in the park, but if anyone could do it, Maggie knew her mother could.

Other than running into Nick at the market, it felt good to be home. The scent of a roast baking, the sound of her mother's humming from the kitchen, even her father with his nose in the paper. She missed all that. Life had gotten too crazy these past few years. She hadn't even realized it until this minute just how crazy.

She was going to enjoy her time here, she resolved. Enjoy her time with Drew and her parents. She'd put the past behind her a long time ago; it no longer existed. There was only here and now.

The doorbell rang again and when she opened the door the past she'd put behind her stood on her parents' doorstep, staring back at her with eyes as black and deep as a forest at midnight.

Two

Nick couldn't remember when he'd ever seen eyes so deep green before. Eyes so big and wide and... nervous?

So she *was* still shy, he thought, and realized that he found it charming. Most of the women he knew always seemed so sure of themselves, confident almost to the point of intimidating. He liked a little hesitation in a woman, a little uncertainty. He especially liked the fact that he was the cause of it.

Smiling, he pulled her credit card out of his pocket. "You lost this at the market. I thought you wouldn't mind, so I booked us a Jamaican cruise. We leave next week."

She stared at him, then blinked and snatched the card out of his hand. "Thank you."

Then she slammed the door in his face.

This wasn't going exactly as he'd planned.

Nick raised his brows and stared at the closed door. The Maggie Smith he remembered might have been shy, but she'd also been sweet.

But then, the Maggie Smith he remembered had also been skinny and drab.

Damn if he wasn't intrigued.

He noticed Mrs. Potts, the Smiths' next door neighbor, watering the bushes that separated their properties. She'd been the dean's secretary the six months he'd spent in Wolf River County Home for Boys, and she'd been old then. When he nodded at her, the frail woman quickly looked away, pretended she hadn't seen that Maggie had just slammed a door in his face.

Maybe Maggie still thought of him as some kind of convict, even though his "visit" at the county boys' home had been twenty years ago. His "offense," a short joy ride with Linda Lansky on her older brother's new scooter, had been harmless, but Bobby Lansky hadn't been the understanding type. Neither had the judge, unfortunately.

But he really hadn't minded going to the home. Lucas and Ian had both been there at the same time, and at least he got fed regularly, and no one ever punched him in the stomach for leaving a jacket on a chair or playing the stereo too loud. Hell, it had been more like a vacation.

But that was a long time ago. He couldn't imagine that was the reason Maggie was so nervous around him.

Frowning, he stared at the front door. Whatever her reason, he should walk away. He had more work than he could handle, and he didn't have time for a timid, high-strung female, even if she was drop-dead gorgeous.

But then, Nick Santos was not a man to walk away from a challenge. And *this* Maggie Smith, whoever she was, was definitely a challenge.

Besides, he was certain that incredible smell emanating from inside the Smith house was roast beef.

What the hell. He rang the doorbell again.

The door flew open, this time with Angela Smith on the other side. "Nicholas Santos! What a pleasant surprise. Come in, come in." She took hold of his arm and tugged him into the entryway. "I haven't seen you since the wedding. Maggie, sweetheart, look who's here. It's Nick!"

From the corner of his eye, behind him, Nick caught a flutter of hands, a waving motion, but when he turned, Maggie stood perfectly still, a tight, thin smile on her lips.

"We ran into each other at the store," he said with a grin, and watched her cheeks flush at his choice of words.

"Why, Margaret Jane, you didn't even tell me. Shame on you." Angela closed the door. "Well, now that you're here, you're staying for dinner and I'll not take no for an answer. I'm sure you like roast beef and mashed potatoes, don't you, Nick?"

Maggie's head snapped toward her mother. "I'm sure Nick already has other plans, Mom."

"I love roast beef." Nick kept his eyes on Maggie, fascinated by the small twitch of distress at the corner of her jaw. A delicate, enticing jaw, that gave way to a long, slender, enticing neck.

She wanted him gone in the worst way. Which only made him want to stay all the more.

He turned back toward her mother and handed her the grocery bag in his hand. "Bud and Joe's was having a special on these. I thought maybe you could use some.''

Angela took the bag and looked inside. ''Green beans. How thoughtful of you, Nick. I actually sent Maggie to the store for some, but she forgot the list.''

He glanced back at Maggie. The blush that had brightened her cheeks only a moment ago now colored her entire face. ''Try them with a can of mushroom soup and cheese,'' he said. ''They make a great casserole.''

''You cook?'' Angela beamed at Maggie. ''He cooks, Maggie. Isn't that wonderful? Boyd—'' Angela stuck her head into the living room ''—Nicholas Santos stopped by to say hello. He's going to have dinner with us. Oh, heavens, I've got to check on the biscuits. Maggie, sweetheart, take Nick out to say hello to your father.''

Nick watched Maggie squirm when her mother left them alone in the entry hall. She stood stiff as a fence post, and he could see her battle between good manners and tossing him out of the house.

Whatever was going on here with the woman, Nick had the distinct feeling it went beyond shyness.

A challenge *and* a mystery. Now if only he could get the lady to talk to him, he just might stand a chance. ''I heard you got married.''

She glanced over her shoulder toward her father. ''Yes, I did.''

Nick frowned. That wasn't the right answer. She was supposed to tell him she was divorced. ''I also heard you got divorced.''

Surprise lit her eyes as she looked back at him. ''Did you?''

Not exactly an answer, but Nick never gave up easily. "I also heard you're a journalist for a New York newspaper. With your own column even."

That brought a lift of one finely arched eyebrow. "You heard all that."

"So are you?"

"A journalist?"

"Divorced."

"Oh. Yes."

He took a step closer. Damn, but she smelled good. "Maybe we could go out for dinner sometime. Catch up on what we've been doing for the past twelve years."

She took a step back. "I don't think so, Nick. I'm just here to help take care of my dad for a few weeks. I won't really have much time."

"Coffee, then." He moved in closer again, drew the scent of her deep into his lungs. "Tomorrow night."

Something caught her ear, the faint sound of laughter, Nick thought. She paled, then grabbed hold of his arm and nearly dragged him into the living room. "Why don't we go say hello to my father?"

Her abrupt change of behavior surprised him, but since she was actually touching him, he decided they were making progress. "How's the leg, Mr. Smith?" Nick asked the back of the sports page.

The paper came down. Boyd Smith still looked the same, though he was bald now over a rim of silver-gray hair. He still had the same scruffy eyebrows and penetrating stare. "You still riding those motorcycles, Santos?"

"Only for pleasure now, sir."

"Got any whisky?"

"Not on me."

'How 'bout a cigar?'

"'Fraid not."

"Next time you come over, see that you bring both."

"Yes, sir."

The paper went back up, and Nick assumed that their talk was over. Not exactly a long conversation, but a productive one. He'd already been invited back. He grinned at Maggie, but she merely frowned. When she realized that she was still holding his arm, she quickly dropped her hand.

"Excuse me." She backed away. "I need to…check on something. Why don't you just have a seat and I'll be back in a—"

"Mommy, my movie's over!"

The flying tackle from a pair of small arms caught Maggie around the knees from behind, sending her sprawling forward into Nick's arms. He caught her smoothly, fully enjoying the feel of her soft body and full breasts against his chest. Much to Nick's delight, she struggled to disentangle herself, which only increased the friction of their bodies.

Her body still flush with his, Maggie looked up at Nick, a mixture of shock and horror in her eyes. She finally managed to wrench herself free, then turned to face the three-foot-high, dark-haired dynamo who'd knocked her off her feet.

"Drew!" Maggie gasped. "I've told you not to do that."

"I forgot." The youngster stuck his hands into the pockets of his jeans and glanced down contritely. "Sorry. I just wanted to hug you."

Nick knew a con job when he heard one. This kid was good, he thought with amusement. And cute, too. Nick knew nothing about children, but he'd guess the boy to be around five or so, with dark, almost black hair nearly the same color as his big, thickly lashed eyes. His oversize feet were encased in thick-soled tennis shoes, and Nick could only imagine he'd be tall as a doorway by the time he was sixteen.

So little Maggie Smith had a kid. How 'bout that.

He watched her kneel beside her son, saw the struggle on her face to remain stern. "Hugs shouldn't hurt, sweetheart. You have to be more careful."

The child nodded, then glanced up. His dark eyes turned wary at the sight of a stranger, but he didn't look away or step back.

Maggie stood stiffly behind her son, her hands on his shoulders as she faced Nick. "Drew..." She hesitated, then pulled in a breath and continued, "This is Nick Santos. Nick, this is my son, Drew."

Nick stuck out his hand, which the child promptly accepted. Nice grip, Nick thought. "How's it going, Drew?"

"You drive a truck?" the boy asked.

Did everyone in this family answer a question with a question? Nick wondered. "Yes, but mostly I ride a motorcycle."

"Motorcycles are cool," Drew said with all the authority of a child, "but I want to drive a truck when I grow up."

"Maybe we can go for a ride sometime, if your mom says it's okay."

"Really?" Drew's eyes brightened. "On the motorcycle or the truck?"

"Either. Both."

"Wow. Really? Can I, Mom?"

Maggie had been vigorously shaking her head, but she went still when Drew looked up hopefully at her.

"I don't think so, honey. You're not big enough for motorcycles yet."

"I'm almost five," Drew complained. "Tommy Fuscoe rides on his daddy's motorcycle all the time, and he's littler than me."

"You're not Tommy Fuscoe," Maggie said firmly. "But we'll see."

A definite no, Nick realized. But with the two of them working on her, Nick was confident they'd change her mind...one of several things he intended to change her mind on.

"Wanna see my bike?" Drew looked at Nick. "My grandpa got it for me just to have here. Didn't you, Grandpa?"

"Needs new tires," Boyd mumbled with a flip of his newspaper.

"C'mon." The youngster sprinted through the front door. "It's in the garage."

"After you." Nick swept his hand out and Maggie moved past him, though she was careful not to brush against him. But the warmth of her body where she'd been thrust against him only a few moments ago still lingered on him, and he was anxious to feel that warmth again.

And next time she fell into his arms, he intended that they be alone.

He caught her arm on the porch, took it as a good sign when she didn't immediately pull away. "Cute kid," he said, wanting a moment alone with her now. "He must look like his father."

She shrugged, then glanced in the direction her son had run, but not before Nick caught the flicker of pain in her eyes. Damn, he thought. She must still be hung up on the guy.

"You see him much?"

Frowning, she looked back at him. "See who?"

"Drew's father. Your ex."

"Oh." She shook her head. "He lives in Vancouver."

He thought of his own father, a man he never knew, then thought of the stepfather he wished he'd never known, and felt an instant kinship with Maggie's son. "That must be hard on Drew."

"He was only a year old when we divorced. He doesn't remember him." She jammed her hands into her pockets and sighed. "Look, Nick, I appreciate you stopping by, but I really would rather—"

Drew's scream stopped her, and she was off the porch running toward the garage in a space of a heartbeat. Nick took the porch steps in one jump and was rounding the side of the house when he heard the sound of a child's sobs from inside the garage.

He found mother and son kneeling beside the bumper of a white compact. Crushed under the right front tire was the back wheel of a child's bicycle.

"You broke it," Drew cried. "You broke my bike."

"Oh, baby, I'm so sorry." Maggie looked up at Nick, her face stricken. "I...I didn't see it."

Nick moved around to the passenger door, put the car in neutral and pushed it backward. Metal creaked as the car's tire rolled off the bike.

Tears streamed down Drew's face as he reached for the handlebars and attempted to stand the twisted bike up. "I'll never ride it now," he railed.

"I'll get you another bike, sweetie." Maggie reached out to touch her son's shoulder, but he shrugged away from her.

"I don't want another bike. This was the best one, and Grandpa gave it to me."

Nick studied the bike and without thinking, said, "I'll fix it."

Drew stopped crying, and both mother and son looked up at him. Good grief, Nick thought. Where had that come from? He'd never fixed a kid's bike in his life.

"You will?" Drew swiped at the tears on his cheeks.

The shop was backed up with two weeks of work, he had a mountain of paperwork to do, but what the hell? "Sure. A bicycle's just a motorcycle without an engine, right? Can't be much different. You can come to my shop and help me. We'll make it good as new. Better, even."

"Better?" Drew's face lit up. "And I can come help? Really? Did you hear that, Mommy? Nick says I can help. I'm gonna go tell Grandma and Grandpa."

In a flash of tennis shoes and blue jeans, he was gone. Her mouth open, Maggie stared after her son, then slowly turned to Nick. "This is very embarrassing. You must think I'm some kind of an idiot."

He smiled, leaned in close enough to see the threads of dark brown in her deep green eyes. "Come out for coffee with me tomorrow, and I'll tell you what I think of you." He'd show her, as well, if she'd let him close enough.

She shook her head, but not before he saw the hesitation. And something else, something wistful and sad. "I'm sorry, Nick. I'm just so busy right now. I really can't."

He was trying to imagine her busy, exciting schedule. No work, home all day with her parents and an almost-five-year-old. "Can't," he asked carefully, "or don't want to?"

Her gaze was steady as she met his. "I'm sorry," she said evenly. "I'm just not interested."

Well, *that* was certainly to the point, especially coming from such a *shy, sweet* girl. The words had even been spoken gently, but were still a direct verbal blow to his pride nonetheless. He nodded, backed off from her. "Can I ask why?"

She dragged a hand through her hair, then sighed. "Like I told you, I'm only here for a few weeks to help my parents, that's all. I didn't come here for—"

He grinned when she hesitated, lifted one brow. "Wild sex?"

Surprise widened her eyes at his outrageous comment. They both knew he was teasing, but still, something passed between them. Something intense and distinctly sexual.

"You think that's what I had in mind, Maggie? Coffee, then wild sex?" He put a hand over his chest and gave her his best wounded look. "I might be fast, darlin', but I'm not easy."

She blushed rosy-red. Damn if he didn't itch to touch her heated skin and smooth his fingers over her cheek.

"I didn't mean to be rude," she said softly. "But like I said, I'm just here for my parents."

For a woman who wasn't interested, she was awfully nervous, awfully tense. And as curious as that made him, he knew when to back off.

For the time being.

"All right, then." He flashed her his best smile, then held out his hand. "How 'bout friends?"

She stared at his hand for a long moment before

slipping her fingers into his palm. "Sure." She smiled weakly. "Friends would be great."

Her skin was smooth against his, soft and warm, and he was certain her fingers shook before she quickly pulled away. There was heat between them, all right, he thought with mild satisfaction. No question about it.

"I'll explain something to Drew," she said. "I'm sure he'll understand how busy you must be at your shop. There's a bicycle repair in town I can call in the morning."

"I didn't offer to fix Drew's bike to get you in bed, Maggie," he said tightly. "Whatever it is you think of me, I haven't sunk that low, yet."

"I'm sorry." Distress narrowed her eyes. "I didn't mean it that way. I just thought you might have spoken before you realized what you were letting yourself in for. I was offering you an out."

"I'll let you know when I need an out." He bent down to study the bike. "I can straighten the wheel, but I may have to order a couple of new parts. Come by my shop tomorrow with the bike and Drew. I'll give you both the nickel tour." He relaxed, gave her a slow, easy grin. "I even promise not to hit on you."

She smiled back, the first real smile he'd managed to lure from her. Her eyes softened and for the first time since he'd plucked her out of that stack of tumbled green beans, the tension between them eased.

Damn if she wasn't even more beautiful when she smiled like that, and damn if he hadn't promised not to do anything about it.

All he had to figure out now was how to get her interested without coming on to her.

This was a first for him, he realized, and brightened at the prospect. It wasn't going to be easy. Even now, in the face of her rejection, all he could think about was pulling her into his arms and tasting that gorgeous mouth of hers.

In the meantime, he thought with a sigh, since he couldn't have what he really wanted, roast beef and mashed potatoes smothered in gravy would have to keep him satisfied.

Three

She couldn't sleep. Hot shower, warm milk, counting sheep, three chapters of a boring book. Nothing had worked. She was wide awake, and no matter how hard she tried, she couldn't stop thinking about Nick.

Dinner with him tonight had been the longest two hours of her entire life.

She'd sat beside him, said grace, then passed him the potatoes as nonchalantly as if he were any other guest at her parents' table for any other dinner.

But it was hardly just any other dinner, and Nick was hardly just any other guest.

He certainly had a healthy appetite, Maggie thought. The way he packed food away, she couldn't believe he wasn't at least twenty pounds heavier. But there wasn't an ounce of fat on the man. She'd discovered that first-hand when Drew had tackled her straight into those strong arms and Nick had held her against his broad chest. He was solid muscle, every last inch of his six-foot-four-inch frame.

Exactly as she remembered him five years ago.

How could he just show up here like this now, throwing her entire life into turmoil?

With a groan she sat and turned on the bedside lamp. Running into Nick at the store had been one thing. That she could have handled. But him showing up here, charming everyone in sight, including Drew, was another matter entirely.

The image of her son placing his small hand in Nick's would be burned in her memory forever.

At that moment she'd felt as if time had stopped, as if the world had stopped and nothing else existed but the two of them. The two men in her life who had changed her the most, both of them unintentionally altering her life forever. And neither one of them had a clue how important they were to her.

When her heart had started beating again, when she'd recovered her ability to breathe, all she could do was watch them, watch them in amazement and disbelief that two such wonderful people had touched her life.

She'd found a calm in that moment. As if she'd been waiting for that moment without even realizing it, and now that it had happened, she felt an incredible relief. She'd also realized she'd been acting like an idiot. There'd been no reason for her to be so afraid of them meeting.

In a hundred years Nick Santos would have no reason to believe that Drew was his son.

How could he, when Nick himself didn't even realize that he'd made love to her?

Sometimes even *she* wondered if she'd dreamed that

night, if she'd simply lost it completely and confused a fantasy with reality. At those moments all she'd have to do was look into her son's eyes, watch him smile and she knew the truth: Drew was Nick's son. Absolutely no doubt about it.

And she'd do everything in her power to be certain that Nick never knew.

The soft light from the table lamp spilled onto the rose wallpaper, and Maggie stared at the delicate patterns of flowers and vines. This had been her bedroom growing up, until the day she'd left ten years ago. Hoping for excitement, she'd chosen a large East Coast university, but had realized soon enough that a plain, painfully shy small-town girl just didn't fit in with the big city. She stuck it out, though, earned her journalism degree, and through a college placement agency found her first job with the *North Carolina Tribune*. Never mind she was making coffee and filing, and no one in the office ever gave her a second look, she had a real job with a real newspaper. She'd vowed to prove herself somehow, make them see she could write the best damn article the *Tribune* had ever seen. All she needed was a chance.

Eight months later, due to a flu epidemic that left two-thirds of the office home in bed, she finally got her chance. A sports assignment. Following the National Motorcycle Championship race that afternoon at the local speedway, she was supposed to interview two-time national champion Nick Santos.

She went straight to the bathroom and threw up.

Of all the assignments, of all the people in the world to interview, fate had given her Nick Santos, the man who'd rescued her from Roger Gerckee when she was thirteen years old. She remembered every wonderful, glorious moment of that day.

She'd been eating lunch alone, as she always did, in the back of the lunch area. Roger had singled her out that day and had been taunting her about her braces, big glasses and curly red hair. She'd managed to ignore him until he snatched her sandwich and threw it in the trash can, but then she hadn't been able to stop the tears of humiliation and anger.

Like a knight on a white horse, Nick Santos suddenly appeared. Vividly she could still remember the fury in Nick's dark eyes, hear the deadly calm in his voice, when he'd told Roger that he shouldn't be wasting food like that, then dumped the bully in the same trash can. The entire school had cheered, and she had fallen hopelessly in love.

She'd never told anyone her feelings for Nick. She would have been the laughingstock of the school if she had. She was different from the other girls. They'd always known what to say, what to wear, how to act. She'd simply never fit in, and falling for a boy like Nick was absurd. Nick was not only older, he was part of the notorious Bad-Boy Trio. A girl had to be fast to hang with Nick, she'd heard in whispered rumors, not to mention gorgeous and ready for a little danger.

Maggie had been none of those things, and the most dangerous thing she'd ever done was sneak in late to algebra class while Mr. Greenbaum, the teacher, had his back turned. She'd resigned herself that bad-boy Nick Santos would never, in a million years, look twice at a girl like her.

So it had just simply been more comfortable, and definitely safer, to immerse herself in books and school projects, and keep her fantasies about Nick to herself.

In those fantasies, she was fast, she was gorgeous, a femme fatale that stole his breath and heart and he wanted only her. She was as bad as he was, and damn good at it. Those fantasies had carried her through high school and college.

Until that day five years, six months ago, when she either had to interview him or lose her job.

She'd watched the race from the stands that day, cheered when Nick won his third national championship, driven to his hotel, then sat in her car forty-five minutes before she'd been able to work up the nerve to go up to his suite and actually knock on the door.

The celebration party of Nick's win was in full swing when she stepped—no, when she was *dragged*—through the door of the elegant suite by a large dark-haired man sporting a ponytail. People packed the room, laughing and talking, hard-rock music pounded from a stereo system, and a blond man dressed in a Hawaiian shirt circled the room pouring champagne. The women were all beautiful, the men rugged and handsome, and Maggie had never felt more out of place in her entire life.

She couldn't do this. She still hadn't seen Nick, and even if he'd seen her, he wouldn't remember her, anyway. He had a different woman on his arm every time the tabloids took his picture. If she left right now, she wouldn't have to suffer the humiliation of him having no idea who she was.

She was already turning to leave, already formulating the lie she'd tell her boss, when the Hawaiian man blocked her way and shoved a flute of champagne at her.

"You here from the hotel?" he asked.

Dressed in her tailored navy blue shirt and blazer,

she could understand why he'd think she was hotel staff. "Well, actually—"

"It's in the bedroom bathroom. I thought someone should look at it, but you don't need to send anyone to fix it until tomorrow."

She tried to explain she wasn't with the hotel, but the noise level had risen considerably when two women grabbed Nick and started to dance with him, and the man leading her toward the bedroom couldn't hear her explanation.

She stumbled at the sight of him dancing with the women. Well, he wasn't exactly dancing, he was sort of watching more than anything. Her heart pounded furiously. He was as handsome as ever, his hair as thick and dark as she remembered, his smile just as dazzling. She couldn't find her voice when Hawaiian Man nudged her into the bedroom, then took off.

Grateful for the quiet, Maggie slipped into the bathroom and closed the door behind her. She stared at the champagne in her hand, held her breath and took a big gulp. The bubbles lingered in her throat, tickling, and though she never drank much, she realized she liked the taste. She also liked the sudden shot of confidence buzzing through her.

Setting her cotton workbag on the bathroom counter, she recovered her handheld tape recorder, turned it on and cleared her throat. "Testing, testing," she spoke into the recorder, cleared her throat and said quietly, "Cottleston, Cottleston, Cottleston Pie, a fly can't bird, but a bird can fly." She listened to the recording, then flipped it off again and closed her eyes as she took another drink of champagne.

When she opened her eyes again, she looked into the bathroom mirror and stared at herself. She could have at least put some lipstick on, tried to do something with her wild hair. She'd just never known what to do when it came to cosmetics and hairstyles. Or maybe it had just never mattered to her. Suddenly it seemed to matter very much.

But there was nothing that could be done about it now. With a sigh, she removed her glasses and turned the faucet on, intending to splash cold water on her face. A stream of water sprayed up at her, drenching the front of her jacket. Gasping, she fumbled with the faucet handle and shut off the water. Looks like she found out what Hawaiian Man had wanted her to look at.

Groaning, she removed her jacket and slipped it into her bag with her glasses, then mopped up the water on the counter and floor with a hand towel. This cinched it for her. She was leaving.

She downed the remaining champagne, drew in a deep breath and slipped out of the bathroom.

Someone had closed the bedroom door to the outside parlor and the bedroom was cloaked in darkness. Maggie had no idea where the light switch was, so she felt her way across the large bedroom. The corner couch, a desk chair, the edge of the king-size bed.

A man's chest.

Startled, she stumbled back onto the bed with a strangled cry.

"Sorry, I didn't mean to scare you." He sat down beside her on the bed. "I thought maybe you were in here."

It was Nick! Maggie could barely breathe. He'd actually seen her? And recognized her? His thigh nudged hers and her pulse turned erratic as a New York taxi driver.

"You did?" Because she couldn't draw air into her lungs, her words had a soft, breathless quality to them.

He slipped an arm behind her. "I heard you wanted to see me."

"Well, I…ah, yes, actually." How clever she was. How professional. Sophisticated, she thought with disgust.

"I don't want to keep you from your party," she said, reaching for her bag that had spilled over somewhere on the floor. Why hadn't he turned the light on? And why didn't she suggest that he do so now?

Because she liked it, she realized. Sitting on a bed in the dark with Nick, with champagne buzzing in her head and the masculine scent of his aftershave deep in her lungs.

"They moved the party to the suite across the hall. There's a football game on and that TV is bigger."

"Well," she said, her voice strained, "I guess bigger is better."

He laughed, and the rich, deep sound of it was like velvet stroking her skin. His finger traced a hot, electric trail up her arm to her shoulders where he threaded his fingers through the ends of her curly hair. "You let your hair grow. I like it."

He noticed her hair? Nick Santos, who hadn't seen her in at least seven years, had really noticed her hair? The buzz in her head increased with his nearness, with his touch. When his hand skimmed up her back, she trembled. "Thank you."

"Relax," he said softly, and she felt his breath on her ear. "I realize it's been a while, but you don't have to be so nervous."

There was a roughness to his voice, a sensual quality that sent shivers up her spine. "I'm not nervous," she lied. "But I know how busy you are and I thought that…well, that maybe we should, uh, get started."

He chuckled quietly, then touched her cheek with his fingertips. "You always did make me laugh."

She wasn't sure how to take that. Did he mean, laugh, like laugh *at* her, or laugh, like she said something funny. But he couldn't mean that. She'd never said more than hello to him.

And when his lips closed over hers, when he wrapped his arms around her and pulled her down on the bed, every thought she'd ever had flew out of her head.

She'd been kissed twice in her life before. Once in the tenth grade by Kevin Hatcher, and once by Brian Whitman, who'd sat next to her in an American history course in her second year of college. But neither kiss had tasted like champagne and pure, unadulterated lust, neither kiss had turned her upside down and inside out. Those other kisses would be like comparing a spark to a raging inferno.

His arms tightened around her, and she melted into that inferno, let herself be swept up in the roaring flames, despite the voice from somewhere deep inside her that told her she shouldn't be doing this.

"Nick," she gasped softly when he moved over her jaw and blazed kisses down her neck, "I don't think—"

"Good—" he nipped at the corner of her ear, then found a soft sensitive spot behind her lobe "—don't think. It feels so much better when you don't think."

He was right. So incredibly right. It felt wonderful. Like nothing she'd ever experienced, and was certain she'd never experience again. How many years had this been her fantasy? Why should she deny herself this?

She was an adult. Twenty-four. Wasn't it time she found out what it was really like to be with a man? And this wasn't just *any* man. This was *Nick*.

She heard a soft moan and was startled to realize it came from her. His hands were everywhere now, on her breasts, her leg, pushing her skirt up and sliding up her thigh. Her skin burned everywhere he touched and when he stroked between her legs, caressed her gently, she felt an ache she'd never known before, a desperate need for him to be closer still.

"You're different," he murmured between kisses.

He was right. She was different. From the first moment he'd kissed her, she was no longer shy little Maggie Smith. She felt like a woman for the first time in her life—a sexy, sensuous woman. She pulled his mouth back to hers, moaned when he unbuttoned her blouse and slipped his hand inside to cup her breast. When he pushed the cotton fabric aside and teased her hardened nipples with his thumb she moaned again, then cried out a moment later when his mouth replaced his thumb.

Nothing could have prepared her for the sensations that rocked her body. Pleasure shot like an arrow from her breast to the most intimate part of her. She arched upward, touching him, whispering his name over and over, until clothes were gone and he was finally where she wanted him to be, where she needed him to be.

There was no pain that she noticed, only intense, unbearable pleasure when he filled her. A pleasure that built as he moved, coiled and tightened until she shattered from the sheer force of it. And then he shattered, as well, she realized, amazed that she could do that.

Her heart was still beating wildly when he pulled her

close and tucked her tightly against him. "Stay with me, Cindy," he whispered, kissing her softly.

Cindy?

Good God, he thought she was someone else.

Humiliation stiffened her body. She couldn't move, couldn't breathe. She simply wanted to be swallowed up whole and never seen again. She lay like that, until she heard the soft, regular sound of his breathing, then slipped out from the bed, quietly gathered her clothes and dressed in the dark.

She was at her car before the pain seized hold of her, halfway home before the tears started. She'd had to pull over to the side of the road and let the torrent rip through her. He'd thought she was someone else, thought he'd made love to someone else in the dark.

Someone named Cindy.

He'd be furious when he found out, she thought frantically. Or else he'd laugh his head off. Either way, she could never face him again. Ever.

But if he thought she was Cindy, then he didn't know whom he *had* made love to, did he? No one had known who she was. The Hawaiian man thought she was from the hotel. She'd never given her name to anyone, and Nick had never actually seen her. He didn't know it was poor little Maggie Smith in his bed, a woman at whom he never would have looked twice.

And he would never know, she resolved. Never.

She went home that night and wrote her article. The editor of the newspaper was pleased enough with her work to give her more assignments, and slowly she worked her way into a permanent column in the Health section of the paper.

Two months later, as she stared at the positive tester for pregnancy in one hand and an article about Nick's paternity suit in the other hand, she knew she couldn't tell him he was going to be a father. He didn't even know he'd made love to her. How could she stand the humiliation of actually trying to prove that he had, only to have him reject her and their child, anyway? He'd wanted no part of her, and he certainly wouldn't want any part of a child.

Nick Santos, whom she'd loved from afar since she was thirteen years old, was the father of her child. She touched her stomach, marveling at the wonder of it all. She'd love this child with every breath, with every beat of her heart. She'd had Nick for only one night, but she'd have his child for the rest of her life. Happiness overflowed, gave her the strength to tell her parents she was pregnant and had no intention of marrying the man, gave her the determination to take control of her life, to gain the confidence she'd never had, and the resolve to let go of the past and forget Nick Santos.

She married Richard, a journalist at the *Tribune*, when Drew was six months old, but they both realized it was a mistake six months later, and the divorce was friendly. She'd been offered a job in New York shortly after that, and one year later she had her own column at the *Times*. Her apartment was small but homey, and close to the park. When she wasn't working and the weather permitted, she and Drew spent most of their time there. She was content with her life, where she'd come from, and where she was going.

She was no longer poor little Maggie Smith. She'd learned more than a few things about life, even learned how to use makeup and what to do with her hair. The glasses had gone in the trash, she wore contacts now, and living in New York had taught her about clothes and style.

She was a new woman, one she liked. A mother and a successful journalist. She didn't need anything else in her life right now. Not a man, and most certainly not Nick Santos.

"So let me get this straight." Lucas Blackhawk leaned against the fire-engine-red toolbox and tipped the soda can to his lips. "You're telling me that Nick Santos, ladies' man, most dedicated bachelor west of the Mississippi, is actually having woman problems?"

"Did I say I was having woman problems?" The wrench in Nick's hand slipped off the exhaust bolt he'd been tightening and skidded across the concrete floor. Nick glared at Lucas. "I never said a damn thing about woman problems. Are you here to help, Blackhawk, or just drink my soda and butt into my personal life?"

"Testy this morning, aren't we?" Lucas took another swallow of root beer and scrubbed at his Saturday-morning beard. "So she said no, huh? Pray tell, who is this woman of such high refinement and intelligence?"

"If you're not going to help," Nick growled, "get the hell out of here. I'm busy."

"I'm helping." Nick reached into a drawer in the toolbox and handed Nick a half-inch wrench. "Just tell me who she is, Nick. I won't laugh at you, I promise."

Nick grabbed the wrench and knelt back down beside the motorcycle. He knew damn well that Lucas wouldn't leave him alone until he found out the name of the mysterious woman. "Margaret Smith," he muttered under his breath.

"What's that you say?" Lucas cupped his ear and leaned closer. "Ingrid Whit?"

"Margaret Smith," Nick snapped back as he settled the wrench on the bolt again. "Maggie Smith."

If he hadn't been so annoyed, Nick would have enjoyed the blank look on Lucas's face.

"Maggie Smith?" Lucas repeated, wrinkling his brow. "You mean, quiet-as-a-mouse, never-looked-anyone-in-the-eye, big glasses and curly red hair Maggie Smith?"

"The same." Only definitely not the same, Nick thought.

Lucas gave a snort of laughter. "Well, no wonder she turned you down, Santos. You asked out a woman with an IQ higher than her shoe size."

The wrench slipped off the bolt again and flew out of his hands. Eyes narrowed, Nick straightened and snatched a rag from his back pocket. "Don't you have a ranch and a wife to go home to, Blackhawk? A pregnant wife?"

"My foreman has a handle on the ranch and besides, Julianna is cranky this morning. Our boys had a soccer game going on in her belly all night. I thought she needed some time alone."

"*I* need some time alone. Get the hell out of here."

Lucas grinned and settled back comfortably against the toolbox. "So other than her apparent good sense and keen judgment, why'd Maggie turn you down?"

Nick ground his teeth together. He'd spent the entire night trying to figure it out. He had a good sense of humor, dammit. Women liked that. He wasn't hard to look at. He'd been told he could be charming.

She was a writer, maybe writer types went for those sensitive guys. Thoughtful, reflective men who read poetry and smoked pipes and sat on top of mountains pondering the universe. Poetry wasn't his thing, he'd take a good cigar over a pipe anyday, and he'd sure as hell rather climb the damn mountain than sit on it.

So maybe he wasn't her type, he admitted grudgingly. But she didn't have to be so narrow-minded, he thought with irritation. If she never tried praline-pecan-chocolate-peanut-butter ice cream, how would she know if she liked it or not? She just needed to give it a try and take the plunge, expand her horizons.

Somewhere around 3:00 a.m. he decided that those horizons were going to include him. When that sky-scraper of green bean cans had fallen on her, he'd saved her from injury and possible concussion. It was his duty, his responsibility to save her from a life of boredom and monotony, as well. For her own good, of course.

Her rejection might have wounded his pride a little, but Nick Santos always bounced back. He always had, he always would. Nothing ever got to Nick Santos that a long motorcycle ride and a cold beer wouldn't cure.

Nick bent and scooped up the wrenches he'd dropped, then turned to Lucas and shrugged. "She's more delicate than most women. I came on a little strong, that's all."

"Nick Santos come on strong?" The surprise was phony, but the grin real. "No."

That did it. "Get out of here, Blackhawk, before I cram one wrench down your throat and the other—"

"Excuse me."

Both men turned at the sound of the sultry voice. Maggie stood in the doorway of the converted ware-house that was now Nick's shop, her hands on her son's shoulders.

Four

"**I** hope this isn't a bad time. You said to stop by."

He simply couldn't find the words to answer her. The outside morning light struck her from behind, lighting up her thick auburn hair like gold fire. She wore it loose, and it fell over the shoulders of her forest-green sweater, a color that matched her eyes. She was positively dazzling.

Lucas was staring, as well, Nick noted with irritation. In fact, if his jaw fell open any wider, it would hit the bottom drawer of the toolbox. "Maggie? Maggie Smith?"

"Hello, Lucas." Maggie smiled. "I'm surprised you remember me."

"I remember Maggie Smith." Lucas managed the good grace to at least close his mouth. "I just don't remember *you*."

"Thank you, I think." She touched the top of

Drew's head. "This is my son, Drew. Drew, this is Mr. Blackhawk."

Lucas pushed away from the toolbox, then knelt down in front of the youngster to shake his hand. "Just call me Lucas."

Drew politely shook Lucas's hand. "Nick came over for dinner last night and my mom ran over my bike and Nick says he can fix it and I can help."

"You don't say?" Lucas grinned widely at Nick. "Well, you came to the right place. Nick can fix just about anything. I'll bet he can even make it go faster. Right, Nick?"

Nick resisted the urge to scowl at Lucas when he grinned widely at him.

"Can you, Nick?" Drew asked. "Can you make it go faster?"

"Sure can, pal." Nick smiled at the boy, his annoyance with Lucas forgotten at the excited expression on Drew's face. So what if Lucas knew he was repairing a bicycle? He was just helping the boy out. It wasn't like he'd gone soft on kids or anything. He liked them well enough, he'd just never been around them, certainly was never expecting to have any of his own. What the hell would he know about being a parent? His own mother split the day before his tenth birthday, and the stepfather she'd left her son with spent more time in bars than the run-down apartment they'd called home.

Besides, he'd have to get married to have kids, and why would he do a silly thing like that? He liked his life just as it was. He was doing exactly what he wanted, when he wanted, with whom he wanted.

Well, at least until Maggie had turned up. If he was doing exactly what he wanted, with whom he wanted, they'd be somewhere alone right now, preferably his bed.

"Wanna see my bike?" Drew asked Lucas, pulling Nick out of his fantasy. "My mom flattened it real good."

"Drew." Maggie blushed. "I'm sure Lucas has things to do."

"Not at all." Lucas took the boy's hand. "Let's go have a look."

They were gone before Maggie could protest. She watched her son drag Lucas out of the shop, babbling the entire time about trucks and motorcycles. Her heart skipped when she turned back to Nick. The man absolutely took her breath away.

He'd rolled the sleeves of his deep blue flannel shirt to his elbows, revealing strong, muscled forearms lightly sprinkled with dark hair. Faded blue jeans fit low over lean hips and long powerful legs. The boots were also well-worn, black, Western-style with a strap across the back. Everything about this man was rugged and masculine and positively sexual.

She knew she was staring, she just couldn't help herself. And he was staring back, with a smug, self-satisfied smile that told her he knew exactly what she was thinking. When the portable phone on his work bench began to ring, he turned away to answer it. She breathed a sigh of relief and wandered through the shop, needing some distance from him as much as being curious about his business.

Clean, was her first thought. The concrete floor shone, the walls had been freshly sprayed with soft-gray paint, sunlight poured through spotless windows that rimmed the upper half of the entire building. Motorcycles in various stages of repair lined one wall, thick tires, racing decals, shiny chrome and polished leather. Even with her inexperienced eye, she could tell they weren't the kind that one would take out for a Sunday ride. They looked sturdier, more powerful, formidable. Not so different from the man, she thought, glancing over at Nick's broad shoulders and tall, muscular body.

She quickly squashed the longing that welled up inside her and forced her attention to the back half of the shop where a corner section had been converted into a spacious office with floor-to-ceiling windows. She strolled inside, caught the scent of strong coffee warming on a corner table that sat beside a desk piled high with mail and newspapers. Racing posters lined one wall, along with photos of Nick on his motorcycle. She moved close and stared at one framed shot of him airborne over a mound of dirt, a flash of yellow racing suit and flying dirt.

"I broke my leg when I landed on that one," he said from behind her. "Put me out of the circuit for six months."

"I remember." She'd fretted over that injury, had asked for an assignment to cover the accident just so she could legitimately call the hospital and check on him. "That was in Colorado."

"Well, well." He sat on the desk beside her, his knee nearly touching her leg. "I wouldn't have taken you for a racing fan."

Stupid, stupid, she cursed herself. "Actually, I'm not." Because her hands were shaking, she slipped them into the pockets of her slacks and forced herself to meet his steady gaze. "I had to sub for a colleague that week who wrote the sports column. Nick Santos breaking his leg was big news, so I covered it."

"You wrote an article about me?" His brows shot up. "What'd you write?"

She could have told him, word for word, every line she'd written. Every adjective, every verb, every noun. "That was almost three years ago, Nick. I've written hundreds of articles since then."

"Gosh, thanks, Maggie," he said dryly. "Remind me to call you whenever my ego gets a little too big."

She almost smiled at his childlike pout. "Based on all these trophies, the calls might get expensive." She glanced down at a notepad-size open phone book on his desk. "It looks like you're already busy enough making calls. Are these all women's phone numbers?"

Nick quickly shut the book. "Just friends."

Friends. She thought of his offer yesterday to be "friends," and could only imagine how his definition of the word differed from hers. Not that it really mattered, she decided. She had no intention of following that line of thought.

He'd scooted forward, and his leg was touching her thigh now. A current of heat arced through her, then scurried through her entire body. She stepped aside casually, glanced over the other photos on his wall with the forced intensity of a student studying fine art. But it was an older picture, a snapshot in a simple black frame, that truly caught her attention.

Three young men, all devastatingly handsome, all with dark hair and wicked smiles. Dressed in a black racing suit, Nick sat on a motorcycle, holding a shiny gold trophy in his hand while he grinned widely at the camera. Lucas knelt in front, a half smile on his lips that didn't quite make his narrowed eyes, and Ian Shawnessy stood in back, arms folded over his broad chest as he stared intently into the camera, his grin serious, but darkly sensual.

Bad boys, every one of them, Maggie thought, and her heart fluttered just looking at them.

She felt him move behind her, felt the heat of his body as he reached over her shoulder to straighten the picture she'd been staring at. "That was six months out of high school. My first win."

The picture was straight now, but his hand lingered on the edge of the frame. She could barely breathe with his body draped over her like it was. He wasn't even touching her, yet she felt consumed.

"Where's Ian these days?" she asked conversationally, amazed that her voice held steady when her insides were shaking.

Nick shrugged, moved away and sat back down on the desk. "Ian moves around a lot. He can be difficult to track down."

"Was he at Lucas and Julianna's wedding?" Now that she could breathe again, she sucked in a deep lungful of air.

"He was out of the country. Business or something."

Was he being vague? she wondered. But when she turned to look at him, her heart skipped. His gaze held hers, as dark as it was intense, the look of a predator, and she had no doubt who the prey was.

Needing a quick distraction, and some distance from the sexual tension vibrating between them, she turned quickly aside and moved to the back corner of the office where a door was ajar. "What's in here?"

"My bedroom."

"Your bedroom?" She turned back with a jerk, before she realized he'd moved up behind her. When she bumped into his chest, his hands went to her shoulders to steady her.

"Wanna see?" he murmured.

"I'll pass." She pushed away from him, but not as quickly as she intended, and certainly not with the cool conviction she'd resolved to portray. "A bedroom in your business. How convenient."

"As a matter of fact, it is. I've been too busy to look for a house, so it was easier to just build a temporary living area. There's even a kitchen. Sure you don't want to see?"

He was teasing her, she was certain of it. Mocking her rejection of him. Chin lifted, she faced him, forced her own tone to be light. "Are you trying to make a move on me, Santos?"

He chuckled, then took her chin in his large hand and grinned down at her. "Sweetheart, you'll know when I'm making a move, and there won't be any 'try' about it. Besides," he said, and his thumb brushed softly over her lips, "I made a promise, didn't I?"

Something dark entered his eyes, and for a moment Maggie thought he was going to kiss her. God help her, she *wanted* him to kiss her. Her lips parted—

"Mommy, Nick, where are you?"

Nick dropped his hand and stepped away. She slowly released the breath she'd been holding, then gulped in another fresh pull of air before she turned to her son. He waved excitedly from the shop entrance.

"We're in here, sweetheart." The shock of what she'd almost done radiated through her, shot her back to reality like a bucket of cold water full in the face.

"Where do you want this fine piece of machinery?" The bike in one hand, Lucas stood behind Drew.

She waited a beat before following Nick out of the

office, waited for her pulse to settle and the heat she felt on her face to cool.

She'd known better than to come here. No matter how many years separated her and Nick, no matter how much she wished things could be different, she could not allow herself to get close to him again.

But for now she had no choice. She saw the joy in her son's eyes. He was the one person in her life she could never refuse. She would do anything for Drew, anything but let Nick Santos back into her heart again.

"Hold the wrench sideways," Nick explained carefully, then covered Drew's small hand with his own. "Fit it onto the nut and push it away from you."

Drew's face screwed up with concentration. When the bolt came loose, he laughed with delight and Nick found himself laughing right along with the child.

"I did it," Drew yelled to his mother. "Mommy, I'm fixing my bike!"

Maggie smiled at Drew from the office. Nick had seen her watching them through the windows, carefully keeping her distance for the past thirty minutes while her son received his first lesson in mechanics. Every time Drew called out his latest accomplishment to her, she'd simply nodded and smiled, but she hadn't stepped out of the office once, hadn't even spoken.

Margaret Smith Hamilton baffled the hell out of him, Nick thought. She was a beautiful, sexy woman. Intelligent, successful at her work, a loving mother. She was way out of his league, hardly the type of woman he normally went for, and still he couldn't stop thinking about her, couldn't stop wondering.

While Drew ran over to show his mother the bolt he'd removed from the bicycle, Nick considered the possibility that he was interested in Maggie simply because she'd turned him down. But in his gut he knew there was much more to his fascination with her than the challenge. Something he couldn't quite put his finger on, a feeling he couldn't identify or define.

He rubbed at the back of his neck, but the feeling didn't go away. It lingered, hung on quietly but tenaciously.

Sex and women had always been comfortable to him and he enjoyed them both, though certainly not to the degree that the tabloids had blasted across their headlines. He might not have been especially choosy with the women he'd dated casually, but the women he'd taken to bed he'd chosen with extreme care. Groupies had never been his style, neither had quick flings or one-nighters. The few close relationships he'd been involved in had always been exclusive, he'd genuinely cared about the woman, and once or twice he'd even considered the possibility of love.

But love, whatever it was, had always evaded him. Love, the kind that rang church bells and cried babies, Nick simply didn't comprehend. No woman had ever gotten that far under his thick skin.

Of course, there was his fantasy woman, the woman who had haunted his dreams for the past five years. A woman with skin as soft and smooth as rose petals, a woman who tasted as sweet as honey and cream. Even her scent still lingered in his mind, delicate, yet strangely exotic.

What a strange night that had been. He'd thought he'd made love to Cindy, his ex-girlfriend. Cindy had always been sweet, but they'd never really had a lot in common. Before he'd even gotten out of bed the next morning, he'd called her to talk about giving it another try, told her that he'd enjoyed being with her again the night before. Cindy had slammed the phone down on him, but not before she'd coolly informed him that she may have been at the party, but she most certainly had not "been with him."

He must have stared at the receiver for a full five minutes before he could even hang up the phone. He'd been drinking, but he certainly hadn't been drunk. How the hell could he have made a mistake like that? He'd never been that careless or negligent when it came to sex. He'd sat on the edge of the bed, his mind racing with scenarios of angry husbands and horrible diseases.

That's when he'd looked at the bed and noticed the faint red spot on the sheets.

Good Lord. His mouth went dry as he stared at the sheet. A virgin? He groaned at the thought, cursed himself, then searched the room for something, anything that might reveal his mystery woman's identity.

But there'd been nothing left behind to tell him who the woman was, only a cassette under the bed with a silly quote about cobblestones or some strange thing.

He'd called everyone at the party he'd known, even friends of friends, but no one remembered anything about her. He'd waited for her to call him. He'd even left a number he could be reached at after they checked out of the hotel. But as mysteriously as she'd come into his life, she vanished again.

That was the one woman, the only woman, who had ever gotten under his skin. He'd dreamed about that nameless, faceless seductress often after that, and though it had been a long time since the last dream, strangely enough, he'd had it again, just last night. It had been the same as always: he couldn't see her face, couldn't speak, and then she vanished, like smoke into the night.

Maybe he only wanted what he couldn't have, he thought with a sigh, watching Maggie ruffle her son's hair and laugh. A mystery woman and a woman who wouldn't give him the time of day.

Still, despite her best efforts to convince him otherwise, he was certain that Maggie was not so indifferent to him. He reasoned it could be wishful thinking, but earlier, in his office, when he'd impulsively touched her mouth with his thumb, he'd watched her green eyes deepen, felt the shudder of breath from her lips. She might not have realized it, but she'd even leaned toward him, as if she'd *wanted* him to kiss her. As if she were asking.

He'd come close, so damn close. If Drew hadn't stopped him, he was certain he would have kissed her. He wondered what she would have done if he had. Would she have opened those sweet lips to him and kissed him back, or would she have slapped him?

Life was chock-full of risks, he thought, and rubbed at his cheek. The risk of a sore jaw might be well worth finding out what Maggie Smith tasted like.

"Come see." Drew took hold of his mother's hand and dragged her out of the office. "Nick says I can put air in the tires, but we gotta get new ones first. Don't we, Nick?"

"That's right, pal." Nick handed the youngster a clean rag. "We'll have her fixed in no time."

Grinning, Drew swiped the rag across his hands, then stuffed it into his back pocket the same way he'd seen Nick do. "Can I ride on your motorcycle now?"

Nick glanced at Maggie. She frowned darkly. "Another time, maybe. And anyway, after a hard morning's work, we need hamburgers and chocolate shakes to build up our strength. My treat.''

''Nick—'' Maggie lifted a hand to protest, but Drew was already bouncing with delight. With a sigh, she let her hand drop and shook her head. ''Nick Santos, what in the world am I going to do with you?''

He'd like to tell her, in explicit detail. But there was a child present, so instead he grinned broadly and wiggled his eyebrows. ''Anything you like, Maggie Smith. Anything at all.''

To his surprise, she laughed. The sound rippled through him like a familiar tune from the past, whispered softly to him like a long-forgotten lyric he'd heard before.

He blinked, and the moment passed. Smiling at his own foolishness, he swept Drew up and carried the giggling child to the washstand in the back of the shop.

And all the while, her heart aching, Maggie stood quietly by and watched them play.

Five

"Thanks for the ride, dear." Two tins of fresh-baked cookies in her hand, Angela Smith slid out of the front seat of the car. "Ruby Peterson is going to drive us home after the bridge game, and your father's already settled in to watch the football game in the bedroom. You just enjoy the quiet."

Quiet was exactly what Maggie didn't need. Quiet gave her too much time to think about things, and about people she didn't want to think about. "Are you sure Drew won't be any trouble?"

"Nonsense. Ruby's bringing Tommy, her grandson. The boys will have a good time playing. Give your mother a kiss, Drew."

The kiss he planted on her cheek was noisy and wet, and Maggie smiled at the pleasure of it, knowing that it wouldn't be long before he'd balk at the idea of goodbye kisses. When she straightened the collar of his cotton shirt, he mimicked her and tugged right back at the neckline of her blue chenille sweater. "Grandma says Tommy is bringing his Robot Rider action cars and that I can play with them, too."

"Just mind your manners, young man." Maggie ruffled her son's hair, loved the feel of the silky strands between her fingers. He bounced out of the front seat of the car before she could kiss him back.

"Oh, Margaret, dear." With a thoughtful frown, Angela stared at the tins in her hands. "You know, I think I've brought way too many cookies for tonight, especially since Martha Wimpleman's on a diet again. Why don't you drop one of these tins by Nick Santos's for me? He enjoyed my chocolate pie so much last week, I'm sure he'll like these, as well."

Maggie knew a setup when she saw one. Her mother hadn't stopped talking about Nick since he'd come over for dinner. About what a handsome, *single* young man he was. But Maggie also knew if she told her mother she wasn't interested, she'd only press all the more.

With an indifferent shrug, Maggie took the tin. "Sure, Mom."

She contemplated tossing the cookies out the car window as she turned down Ridgeway Road and headed toward Nick's shop, but she couldn't bring herself to litter or waste food. She thought about eating them all herself, but then she'd only end up with a stomachache.

She didn't want to see Nick, darn it. She'd already seen way too much of him. The visit last Saturday, then ice cream in town at Judy's Creamery. That had been the worst. Watching Drew laugh with Nick and argue over what was better—chocolate with marshmallows and caramel, or vanilla with blueberry bubble gum. They both teased her over her own bland selection of vanilla dipped in chocolate.

She felt as if she were in a vise. Every time Nick looked at her with those dark eyes, every time he smiled, that vise tightened another notch.

That's why she didn't want quiet, why she didn't want to think. With the quiet came the image of him touching her in his office, his fingers on her chin, the gentle caress of his thumb on her lips. Lips that still tingled. Lips that ached to be kissed.

How could she resist him? And even worse, did she truly want to?

She stared at the tin of cookies as if it were filled with snakes. A note. That's it. She'd write a note and just leave it by the front door. He'd find them in the morning.

Satisfied with that solution, she pulled into the parking lot of his shop and turned off the engine. His truck was in the back corner, but that didn't mean he was there. He rode his motorcycle most of the time. Either way, she'd sneak in and out and never be seen. She quickly scribbled a note on a scrap of paper from her purse and stepped out of the car.

The night was warm, and a breeze carried the scent of coyote mint from a nearby field. A crescent moon shone brightly overhead, and the sky was clear, sparkling with thousands of stars.

As much as she enjoyed living in New York, with all its energy and vibrancy, the sky seemed higher here, the trees taller and the stars brighter. There was so much she missed about small-town life. The sense of community, the slower pace. The only horn she'd ever heard honk since she'd come back to Wolf River was

Ethel Myers's attempt to shoo a loose cow out of the middle of the highway.

Several times she'd thought about moving back. She could do free-lance work, or even take a job with a local newspaper. Her work had felt stale to her lately, and the constant chaos in her busy office ground on her nerves like knuckles on a cheese grater. She'd needed this leave of absence, not just for her parents' sake, but for her own. The deadlines had been getting to her lately. The faster she worked, the more assignments they gave her, with tighter deadlines. And even more than all that, she missed her parents, wanted her son to see his grandma and grandpa all the time, instead of phone calls and letters.

But coming back had only been a dream, a fantasy. She could never come back now. Not with Nick here.

The front door to his shop was open a few inches, the lights were on inside. A song blared from a radio, about Hollywood Hills and Hollywood nights and Nick's deep voice sang along. She smiled at his enthusiasm for the song, and in spite of herself couldn't resist peeking her head inside.

He stood over a workbench, a screwdriver in one hand and a carburetor in the other. At least, she thought it was a carburetor. Because she was single, she'd had to learn a little about cars and mechanical things, but she still couldn't say what the difference was between an axle and a piston.

She allowed herself a moment to watch him, to let her gaze linger on the dark waves of thick hair, the stretch of black T-shirt over wide, strong shoulders, the hug of faded denim over a fine rear end and Texas-long legs.

Her pulse ricocheted, her breath quickened. Just

looking at him aroused her, made her want things she knew she could never have.

She started to set the cookies down inside the door when he turned sharply. The irritation in his frown slowly turned to a smile.

Darn, darn, darn.

She couldn't very well just run off now, not without looking completely ridiculous. And she'd certainly done that often enough when it came to Nick.

Be calm, Margaret, she repeated over and over.

He set the screwdriver down and reached for a rag, wiped his hands with it. "Well, well, Maggie Smith. What brings you to the wolf's den?"

She prayed he wouldn't notice her knees were shaking as she walked across the shop. "My mother thought you might like some cookies."

He kept his eyes on her when she handed him the tin. "I'd love some cookies."

Why did he have to keep looking at her like that? As if he wanted to gobble her up whole instead of the cookies? And why was she thinking that she wanted him to?

"Well," she mumbled and backed away, "I have to get going."

He reached out and took hold of her arm. "At least stay and have one cookie with me. I hate to eat alone."

Don't do it, Maggie... "Well, just one."

While he washed his hands, she wandered over to a motorcycle beside his workbench. It was beautiful. A big, powerful-looking machine with polished chrome and a brand-new black leather seat. The only thing missing was an engine.

"Is this yours?" she asked when he came back.

"A friend's. We used to race together." He broke

open the tin, and a smile of pure ecstasy curved his lips. He closed his eyes and breathed in deeply. "Ah, chocolate chip."

He already had half a cookie in his mouth when he offered one to her. "I think I just died and went to heaven," he moaned around the bite.

"I'll tell her you said so." The expression of pleasure on Nick's face bordered on sexual, and Maggie felt her insides shift. She looked quickly away, turned her attention to the motorcycle while she nibbled on a morsel of chocolate. "Why did you quit racing?"

Well into his second cookie, he shrugged. "It was time. I was on the road all the time. Too many different hotels and restaurants."

"And women?" Cursing her loose tongue, she bit the inside of her mouth and felt the warm spread of a blush on her cheeks.

His grin was wide and slow. "You read too many tabloids, Maggie."

"I'm sorry. I shouldn't have said that. It's none of my business."

"I have no secrets." He set the cookie tin down on the workbench and moved behind her. "How 'bout you, Maggie Smith?" he whispered, his mouth inches from her ear. "What are your secrets?"

What are your secrets? His question made her heart stop, but his closeness made it start up again at lightning speed. Her secrets she could never tell him. She watched, mesmerized as he lifted her hand to his mouth, then bent down and sank his teeth into her cookie. Her mouth actually watered.

When he came back for the last bite, and his lips touched her fingers, pleasure rocketed through her. "Let's take a ride." His hands slid to her waist.

"A ride?" she repeated lamely. She could barely think, let alone refuse him.

"Have you ever been on a motorcycle?" He eased her closer to the bike.

She shook her head, felt the hard, cold steel against her leg.

He smiled. "Then your first time will be with me. I like that."

He had no idea how true his words were, or the longing that swelled in her heart. "There's no engine," she pointed out.

"We don't need an engine."

She let out a squeak when his hands circled her waist and lifted her. Instinctively she swung her leg over the bike and grabbed for the handlebars. He climbed on behind her and settled his hands on her hips. "You're in control, Maggie. Feel the power."

She did feel it. It surged through her like a speeding train, made her head spin and her heart pound. He'd sucked her into the fantasy, and she couldn't stop herself. A delicious bubble of forbidden delight swelled inside her. How long had it been since she'd given in to the emotions, just let herself go, let herself *feel?*

Since the last time he'd touched her, she realized.

"Where shall we go?" she asked breathlessly.

"We'll go anywhere you want to, sweetheart. As far and as fast as you like."

His words thrilled her. She closed her eyes, let the sensations course through her. He slid her body snugly against his, wrapped his arms around her waist and held on.

"It's dangerous to ride without a helmet," she whispered, then felt the rise of heat on her cheeks at the innuendo.

He laughed softly. "I won't let anything happen to you. You're safe with me."

Even in her dazed state, she knew that wasn't true. She could never be safe with Nick, but somehow, at the moment, it didn't seem to matter.

She could almost feel the wind in her hair and on her face, the vibration of the powerful engine between her legs. The radio played a hard-rock beat, and the pulse of the music pounded into her blood.

And then there was Nick.

She smelled the soap he'd washed his hands with, something citrus, but his own scent, pure male, consumed her. With a sigh of surrender, she melted into the heat of his broad chest, luxuriated in the strength of his muscular arms.

"Maggie, sweet Maggie," he murmured.

How many times had she dreamed he'd say her name like that? That she might hear *her* name on his lips, not another woman's?

"Don't hold back." His breath fanned her ear and waves of pleasure pulsated through her. "Just let yourself go."

She thought she heard the roar of the engine, but it was the blood pounding in her head. They were going much too fast. It frightened her. It excited her.

She gasped when he nipped gently on her earlobe. "There's a stop sign ahead."

"There's no one around for miles." He brushed his lips over a spot just below her ear, and she shivered in response. "You don't have to stop."

God help her, she didn't want to. She wanted this feeling to last forever. That last tiny portion of her mind that was still rational knew it couldn't, of course, but why not enjoy just a few minutes of heaven?

On a moan, she let her head fall backward. A trail of fire followed his mouth over her neck, then up her jaw. His touch turned her inside out, exposed every raw nerve. And still it wasn't enough.

"Maggie." His voice and breath were strained. "I want you."

She simply couldn't breathe, couldn't think. She turned toward him, needing to stop this, to stop him, but his mouth closed over hers and every word scattered like leaves in the wind.

She tasted like chocolate, Nick thought. Rich and dark and sweet. He angled his head so that he could taste her deeper, felt an arrogant pleasure from her soft whimper of delight. She was interested in him, all right, in spite of what she wanted him to believe. He had no idea why she fought against it as hard as she did, but he intended to break down every defense until he found out.

She murmured a complaint when he moved back to her neck, then trembled when he slid his hands under her soft sweater and cupped her breasts. They were smooth and firm and warm in his palms, encased in delicate lace.

She arched into him, called out his name, and it felt as if a furnace door had blown open inside him. A blast of fire ripped through him, a need so intense that he thought he might explode from its force.

Her nipples were hard against his thumbs, and he wanted to taste her there, to pleasure them both, but the angles of their bodies prohibited it. Frustrated to the point of pain, he tightened his hold on her, and nestled his arousal firmly against her bottom.

"This is what you're doing to me, Maggie," he said harshly. "Tell me what I'm doing to you."

"You're destroying me."

He felt, as well as heard, the anguish in her quiet words. Why did he have the distinct feeling she didn't mean that in the most positive way?

She was as aroused as him, he was certain of that. But there was something she was holding back, something that went deeper than the physical.

She shuddered once, then went still.

"I'm sorry." Dragging a shaky hand through her tousled hair, she sighed, then slid off the motorcycle and met his confused gaze. Her lids were heavy with desire, her lips swollen and still-moist from his kisses. "I can't do this."

There was fear in her eyes, he realized. A look damn close to terror. "Why are you so afraid of me?"

She folded her arms, hugged them tightly to her. "It's not you I'm afraid of, Nick." She drew in a deep breath, then said quietly, "It's me."

That was one answer he certainly hadn't expected. Frowning, he shook his head. "I don't understand."

"I'm going back to New York in a few weeks. I'm sorry if I led you on, but I'm not interested in this kind of—" she hesitated, obviously searching for the right words "—relationship."

"What the hell is that supposed to mean?" The woman had completely devastated him and now she stood here and soft-pedaled what had happened. He wanted to throttle her almost as much as he wanted to kiss her again.

"It means I'm not interested in a one-night stand. It's not my style, Nick."

He narrowed his eyes. "And you think it's mine?"

"Yes."

He let the sting of her answer pass, then pressed his

lips tightly together. "Don't believe everything you read, Maggie."

Between the need still drumming through his body and his sudden irritation, distance between them seemed like a good idea. He stepped off the motorcycle and moved to his workbench to turn off a pounding Rolling Stones song.

Silence echoed in the high ceilings and dark corners.

"Tell your mother I said thanks for the cookies." He looked at Maggie, saw the desire that still burned in her eyes, and he had to turn away. He picked up a screwdriver and focused his attention on the carburetor he'd been rebuilding. "I should have the parts for Drew's bike day after tomorrow. I'll call you."

He stiffened when he heard her move toward him. If she got too close, if she touched him, he wasn't sure what he'd do. Still, he wasn't certain if he was relieved or disappointed when she moved back again.

"Just let me know how much I owe you," she said quietly.

"I intend to. Good night, Maggie."

He didn't look back, not when he heard the door close behind her, not even when he heard her car start up and drive away.

Rather than damage the carburetor, he kicked his toolbox, then threw the screwdriver. It smashed against the metal wall and clattered down behind a stack of tires three deep. Unless he moved thirty tires he wouldn't be using that screwdriver for a while.

Dammit, anyway, the woman infuriated him.

He'd be lying to say his irritation wasn't partly because she wouldn't go to bed with him. Physically she frustrated the hell out of him.

But what really got to him was her presumption of

his morals, or rather, his lack of them. He'd been accused and judged without facts before, dozens of times, and he'd never much given a damn. Even that annoying paternity suit a few years back and what people had thought of him hadn't bothered him. The woman had been out for a little money and publicity for her acting career. He'd still had to prove it to the courts. And while it might be easy to prove you *had* slept with someone, it sure as hell wasn't an easy thing to prove you hadn't.

His entire life, the only people whose opinion of him had ever really mattered were Lucas Blackhawk and Ian Shawnessy. He felt nothing for the mother who'd run out on him, nothing for the drunken stepfather she'd left him with. They were both gone now, his mother he had no idea where, nor did he care, and his stepfather had drunk himself into an early grave.

Lucas and Ian were his only family. They'd always been there for him, and he knew they always would. He trusted them with his life. What anyone else had ever thought of him simply hadn't mattered.

Until Maggie.

With Maggie it mattered.

He just didn't understand why. Why she had him pacing his shop when he had so much work to do. Why he thought about her constantly, found himself in a tangle of sheets every morning since he'd seen her at the market. Why he could still taste her, smell her as if she were standing beside him.

And why, in the fact of absolute rejection, he still wanted her, still couldn't stop thinking about her.

There was something about her that eluded him, like a dream he'd forgotten. She seemed...familiar. Not from when they were teenagers, but something else. Another time. Another place.

Weird, he thought, dragging a hand through his hair. The whole thing was just plain weird.

One block away from Nick's shop, Maggie had to pull the car over to the side of the road. Her hands were shaking too badly to drive. Her entire body was shaking, for that matter.

Why had she let him get so close? She'd known the results would be disastrous if they were alone together. He didn't even have to touch her to make her bones melt. A simple look from Nick was all it took to turn her into a quivering mass of need.

Damn!

She laid her head against the steering wheel, drew in deep breaths to calm herself. She couldn't be mad at Nick, but she was furious with herself. She had to deal with this, deal with her feelings for him. They'd known each other since they were children. He lived in Wolf River now, and even though she would be going home to New York, she'd still have to see him every time she came back here. With her parents getting older, she'd already decided that her visits were going to be more frequent.

She couldn't run every time she saw him. She wouldn't. She wasn't that timid young girl she'd been, growing up. She was a woman now, a mother. Independent and confident.

Slowly she lifted her head, stared into the darkness outside the car with the first sense of calm she'd had since she'd run into Nick at Bud and Joe's and knocked over a tower of green beans.

She wouldn't be afraid; she wouldn't run. She

couldn't live that way anymore. She faced every other problem in her life and dealt with it. She would face her feelings for Nick, as well.

There was no possible way he could ever learn that Drew was his son. As long as she remembered that, she had nothing else to worry about.

Six

"**M**aggie, you look wonderful! I can't believe it's really you!"

Maggie had barely stepped into the door of the Four Winds restaurant before Julianna Hadley—no, it was Julianna Blackhawk now—had her locked in a hug, though the beautiful blonde's advanced pregnancy forced Maggie to rock backward on her heels.

"Oh, my gosh!" Julianna pulled away, blue eyes wide as she covered her mouth with her hand. "I can't believe I said that. I didn't mean, that is, I wasn't—"

"It's all right." Laughing, Maggie gave Julianna's hand a reassuring squeeze. "I do look different. Amazing what a little makeup and a decent hairdo will do."

Taking Maggie's arm, Julianna led the way to their table, asking how Maggie's mother was and if her father was doing well after his surgery. Soft strains of Mozart floated through the elegant dining room as the women walked through, turning several male heads of the business lunch crowd that filled the popular hotel restaurant. The hotel and restaurant was owned by none other than Lucas Blackhawk himself, Maggie had been told by her mother, though now that he was back in the ranching business, the hotel was up for sale.

Apparently, Maggie thought, she wasn't the only one with changes in her life. But still she'd been surprised when Julianna had called and asked her to lunch. They might have been in the same grade, shared several classes, but Julianna and she had never been friends. They had been two completely different people. While Maggie had been shy and dowdy and without friends, Julianna had always been the rich, beautiful Ice Princess—as she'd been cruelly dubbed—and also without friends. But this Julianna was genuinely warm and friendly, and though it hardly seemed possible, even more beautiful.

"I absolutely love that hairstyle on you, Maggie. It's perfect for your face." Julianna eased her body into a corner booth. "You look radiant. Poised and completely self-confident. Life as a famous New York journalist obviously suits you."

Maggie might have argued the compliments, most certainly the famous part, but a waiter in a black tuxedo appeared, snatched the linen napkin from her china plate and flicked it onto her lap in one fluid sweep. When he started to reach for Julianna's napkin, she grabbed it off the table.

"Oh, Henry, for heaven's sake. It's just me. Besides, I haven't got a lap to put this on, anyway, and I don't appreciate having that thrown in my face."

She delicately tucked the napkin under the collar of her white silk blouse, then leaned forward and whispered to the waiter, "I want a chance to win my five bucks back, buster. Next time it's five-card draw instead of stud poker."

A mischievous twinkle in his gray eyes, the waiter leaned forward and whispered back, "Call any game you like, sister. I'll still beat your behind."

With a sniff she settled back into the booth with all the grace of a princess, albeit a very pleasant one. "We'll have two sparkling waters in champagne glasses, please. We're celebrating a reunion here."

"Right away, Mrs. Blackhawk."

His tone might have been solicitous, but Maggie caught the wink of the waiter's eye before he turned away. "I, ah, take it you know him."

"Henry's a regular at Lucas's Tuesday-night poker game. The whole guy thing. Beer, cigars, lots of bragging and cursing. They grumbled about me joining them at first, including Lucas, but I won, of course. Now the cigars are outside and the cursing is at a minimum, except for when I lose. Lucas threatened to wash my mouth out with soap last week."

With a small laugh she rubbed a hand over her ample stomach. "I wasn't about to miss out on all the fun. At least not until the babies are born."

This was *definitely* not the Julianna that Maggie remembered. "Never in a hundred years would I have pictured Julianna Hadley playing poker."

"Julianna Hadley never would have, but Julianna Blackhawk would." A soft smile curved her lips as she touched her stomach. "Children and a husband had been a fantasy for me. I still can't believe it. Me, Julianna Hadley married to Bad-Boy Blackhawk, of *the* notorious Wolf River Bad-Boy Threesome."

Maggie couldn't help the twinge of jealousy that

centered deep in her heart. She was happy for Julianna and Lucas, she truly was. But her happiness for them still didn't stop the ache in her chest, or the longing for something she could never have.

"Oh, listen to me, going on like that." Julianna dabbed at her eyes. "Tell me about your son. Nick says he's got a killer smile."

The thought of Drew lightened the heaviness. He did have a killer smile. His father's smile. Unable to resist, Maggie pulled out her son's preschool and last-season soccer game pictures. "His name is Andrew, after my grandfather, but we call him Drew. He'll be five in three months."

"Oh, Maggie, he's gorgeous." Eyes wide, Julianna stared at the pictures. "Nick was right. This boy is going to break hearts. His father must be very easy on the eyes."

Very easy on the eyes, Maggie thought. It was her heart he was hard on. With a stiff smile, she tucked the pictures back into her wallet.

"I've said something wrong." Julianna closed her eyes and groaned. "Oh, God, I'm such an idiot. I'm sorry, I wasn't thinking. You're divorced."

Maggie could hardly tell Julianna that she'd been thinking of Nick Santos, not her ex-husband. "You're not an idiot, and besides, it was an amiable split."

"But you're still in love with him, aren't you? You had that look there for a moment. And here I am going on about how happy Lucas and I are." Julianna bit her bottom lip. "I'm so sorry."

A shot of panic rang through Maggie. For a moment she thought that Julianna meant she was still in love with Nick. But of course she wasn't, she didn't know about Nick. No one knew. Still, Maggie realized that she'd let her guard down while looking at Drew's pictures. From now on, especially around Julianna, she was going to have to be very, very careful.

Maggie laid her hand on Julianna's. "You have nothing to be sorry for. And no, I'm not still in love with my ex-husband," she said truthfully. "That part of my life is behind me now."

The waiter appeared with the sparkling water and menus and glided off again. Julianna reached for her glass. "Well then, here's to the present and the future. Or as Killian Shawnessy, via Nick Santos, said on the night of my first marriage to Lucas, 'May you never forget what is worth remembering, or remember what is best forgotten.'"

Maggie's mother had relayed most of the story concerning Julianna and Lucas, how Lucas had suddenly returned to Wolf River, then shocked the town by marrying Julianna in the courthouse a few days later. Gossip flew hot and heavy for several weeks, no one expected them to last, until several weeks later when they were married again, with nearly the entire town in attendance. Maggie had heard, down to the color of the centerpiece roses and the chocolate filling in the wedding cake, every romantic detail of the reception that Lucas had surprised Julianna with, how nearly every woman there had swooned when he kissed his wife after repeating their vows. No one questioned their love after that day. True love, lasting love. The kind that time and adversity only strengthens.

Maggie thought about Julianna's toast. *Never forget what is worth remembering, never remember what is best forgotten.* She'd managed to accomplish half of that with Nick: she'd remembered every beautiful mo-

ment they'd shared. She just couldn't quite forget the
unpleasant part.

But she would. She'd vowed to put the past behind
her, to let go of her feelings for Nick and simply move
on with her life. That's exactly what she intended to
do. That's what she had to do.

"We're having a small celebration Saturday night in
honor of Blackhawk Ranch reopening," Julianna said.
"I'd love for you to come."

Knowing that Nick would be there, Maggie started
to decline, then stopped herself. Hadn't she resolved to
deal with Nick? To simply face him and overcome her
feelings? How else was she going to move on with her
life?

"I'd love to come." Maggie lifted her glass. "Now
I'd like to make a toast. To old friends and new beginnings."

New beginnings, Maggie repeated silently as they
clinked glasses. Her life was starting over again as of
right now. The past was the past, and it no longer existed.

Smiling, she sipped her water, then settled back into
the booth. "Now, Mrs. Blackhawk, tell me more about
this wonderful hunk you've married."

Two days later Maggie's "new beginnings" started
to crumble at exactly 6:45 p.m., the precise minute that
Nick called and told her he'd be at her house at seven-
thirty to pick her up for the party. The telephone dial
buzzed in her ears before she even had a chance to say
no.

Not that the word *no* had stopped him before.

She stared at the receiver, thought about calling him
back, then decided there was no time like the present

to confront him. Things had gotten out of hand three nights ago, but that wasn't going to happen again. Tonight she was determined to have control.

Besides, this wasn't a date. He was giving her a lift to the party, that was all. It wasn't as if they were *together*.

And even more important, they wouldn't be alone.

The fact that she took a little extra care with her hair and makeup had nothing to do with Nick, she told herself. The fact that she wore her black silk suit and pearls—that had nothing to do with Nick, either. There would be people at the party she hadn't seen in a long time. She wanted to look nice, that was all.

When the doorbell rang at seven-thirty, the pearl earring in her fingers slipped and bounced into the bathroom sink. She scrambled for it, narrowly catching it before it slid down the drain. She heard her mother's hellos, her father's welcoming grunt, then her son's enthusiastic greeting.

"Maggie, dear," her mother called, "Nick's here. I'm on the phone in the kitchen, but come say goodbye before you leave. Boyd, you better not be sitting in your chair. You still have three more hallway laps to finish on your crutches."

Her hand was shaking as she slid the earring in place and secured it. Her skin felt tight, her palms were damp. Lips pressed tightly together, Maggie stared at her reflection. *You're not little Maggie Smith anymore,* she scolded herself.

Tonight was the night to prove to herself, and to Nick, what she was made of.

Three deep breaths and she felt much calmer. She intended to have a good time tonight, and not even Nick Santos was going to stop her.

She passed her father in the hallway and kissed him on the cheek. He grumbled something about slave drivers and stupid doctors, then looked her over and gave her a wink of approval.

Drew, ready for bed in his Hercules pajamas, sat cross-legged on the floor in the living room. Wearing a black blazer and white polo shirt with black dress jeans and boots, Nick hunkered down beside him, watching while Drew demonstrated the fire power of his brand-new Robot Rider supersonic tank. Both thick, dark heads of hair were bent over the toy in rapt attention.

Maggie's heart tripped. How could he not see? she wondered. How could *everyone* not see that this little boy was Nick Santos's son?

"Target locked on," Drew said in his best Robot Rider Commander voice. "Ready, aim, fire!"

The lipstick-size foam rubber missile struck her square in the forehead. Drew's eyes widened in shock, waiting for the firm reprimand against flying objects in the house.

Nick's eyes also widened, then narrowed with a dark intensity that sizzled up her spine and made her wish her skirt wasn't so short.

"Sorry, Mommy." The apology was sincere. "Boy, you sure look pretty!"

Stunning is the word that came to Nick's mind. Breathtaking. He quite literally had to remind himself to breathe. Shimmering in black stockings and high heels, her legs went on forever. Her suit, black silk edged with velvet, hugged her hips and waist, showed every tempting curve of her slender body. She'd swept her hair up in a fiery mass of curls, and several wayward strands whispered over the string of pearls circling the base of her neck.

He tried to swallow, but he'd forgotten how.

"Thank you, Drew. Hello, Nick." Her eyes, a deep smoky green, leveled with his as he rose from the floor.

She smiled slowly, sensuously, the confident relaxed smile of a woman who knew exactly the effect she had on men and wasn't afraid of it.

Yet another side to Maggie Smith, Nick thought dimly. And while he definitely liked *this* Maggie, this poised, self-assured femme fatale, he wasn't certain his heart could take it.

When she glided into the room and he caught the scent of her perfume, something erotic and mysterious, he was certain he was a goner.

And what a way to go.

"Excuse me," he said after clearing his throat. "I'm supposed to pick up Maggie Smith. Could you please tell her I'm here?"

Drew started to giggle. "Silly. That's my mom right there. She just looks different 'cause she's got clothes on."

From the mouths of babes, Nick thought. A wide grin accompanied his long, slow glance, and a sudden, intense desire to know what she wore under those clothes heated his blood. Black lace, he decided, and his fingers twitched imagining what it would feel like under his hands.

"Well, now," he drawled, "it *is* your mom, isn't it? For a moment there, I thought she was someone else."

"Like who?" Drew asked.

Nick rubbed his chin and looked Maggie over again, punched back the raw lust rolling in his gut. "Mrs. Peterson, the librarian, maybe?"

Maggie rolled her eyes at his nonsense. Drew shook his head. "Mrs. Peterson plays bridge with my grandma. She wears big glasses and walks with a limp."

Nick nodded with agreement. "I forgot about the limp. Well, how about Mrs. Wimpleman?"

Drew burst into giggles. "Mrs. Wimpleman has three chins and laughs like a chicken."

"Drew," Maggie warned.

"It's true." All innocence, Drew looked up at Nick. "Grandma says every time Mrs. Wimpleman laughs, they check under her chair for eggs."

"That's enough." Maggie frowned at her son, but Nick saw the twitch of a smile in the corner of her soft, red lips. She bent to kiss her son's cheek, then wiped away the faint smudge of lipstick with her thumb. "You go get in bed now. Grandpa's going to read you a story."

"Delbert Dragon's Talent Show!" he yelled and ran down the hall.

Maggie reached for her coat and sighed. "What else? They've only read it the past four nights."

"I hear kids like to know what's going to happen next." Nick held Maggie's coat, smoothed his hands over her shoulders after she slipped it on. "Personally," he whispered in her ear, "I like a little mystery."

She moved away from him, but not before he breathed in the warmth of her scented skin. Not before he felt her tremble.

Maggie said goodbye to her mother, but when they stepped out on the porch, she touched his arm. "Nick, I appreciate you picking me up, but I want you to understand that this isn't, I mean, that we're not... together this evening."

We'll see about that. He smiled easily. "Do you have other plans?"

She sighed with exasperation. "That's not what I mean."

"What *do* you mean?"

"I just mean that we're not *together.*"

"Oh. So you mean, like—" he traced his finger over the lapel of her coat "—you're a free agent?"

"Something like that." Her voice faltered. "Stop that."

"Stop what?"

"Stop…touching me like that."

"How would you like me to touch you?" he murmured, leaning close.

She swayed toward him, then blinked. With a frown she brushed his hand away. "I'm serious, Santos. We're going to this party strictly as friends. Remember that." She turned on her pretty heels and headed for his truck.

They might be going to the party as friends, he thought with a smile as he followed her. It was how they came home that was important.

A bottle of beer in his hand, Nick leaned against a back porch rail decorated with tiny white lights and watched the steady stream of guests moving into Lucas and Julianna's backyard. Along with half the town of Wolf River, there were several cattle ranchers and horse breeders in attendance, as well. An exhibition of Lucas's new stock was planned for later, and based on the tension in the air among the buyers, the competition was going to be fierce.

Steaks and ribs grilling on smoky barbecues filled the air, and a caterer's spread that gave new meaning to the term *Texas-size* stretched across long, linen-covered tables. Drinks flowed freely, served by pretty girls in short Western skirts and boots, and country-western music from a six-piece band had the dance floor nearly full.

Lucas came out of the house and spotted Nick in the shadows of the porch. "Hey, Santos, you hiding back here?"

"Not very well, I guess." Nick tipped his beer to his mouth and nodded at Lucas. "Monkey suit looks good."

Lucas frowned darkly and tugged at his tie. "Julianna likes it. Wanna make something of it?"

Nick grinned. There was nothing he'd like better than a round with Lucas to ease the tension brought on by a certain redhead. "Love to, but I figure I'll wait until after I try out some of those snacks over there and drink up all your beer. Won't be much reason to stay after that, unless I get to steer your beautiful wife around the dance floor just to make you jealous."

"I've got two sons to kick you square in the gut if you get too close." Lucas waved a bottle of beer from a passing waitress and settled back against the railing. "Besides, I thought you were here with Maggie."

"We're not *together*," Nick said sourly and tossed back another long swallow. Where the hell was she, anyway? Julianna had pulled her away the minute they'd walked in the door and he hadn't seen her since.

Lucas's brows shot up. "Well, I'll be damned. You really do have a thing for her."

"I haven't got any *thing* for anybody," Nick snapped. "We're just friends."

Lucas gave a bark of laughter. "Nick Santos, *friends* with a beautiful woman? This I gotta see."

"Don't make me embarrass you in front of all your guests, Blackhawk." He scanned the crowd again, frowned when he caught sight of a familiar male blond head with a pretty brunette. "What the hell is Gerckee doing here?"

"Roger?" Lucas narrowed his gaze on their school days bully-turned-lawyer. "Damn. He must have come with Jennifer Hart, the new manager I hired at the Four Winds. She doesn't know what a scumbag Roger is yet."

"I thought you sold the Four Winds."

"Still entertaining offers, as we say in the world of high finance. I've funneled all my other holdings into this ranch and some overseas investments. Once the hotel is sold, I'm a full-time rancher."

"And full-time daddy," Julianna said, slipping her arms under her husband's as she kissed his cheek. "Mrs. Peterson says you promised her a dance and she's looking to collect."

Lucas searched the dance floor and spotted the elderly librarian. "We could escape now, just you and me, darlin'. No one would miss us."

"No one except Mrs. Peterson. Ah, here she comes now."

Lucas glanced at Nick imploringly. "Say, Nick—"

"Not a chance, pal. Friendship only goes so far."

With a grin, Lucas slapped Nick on the back. "And in your case, Santos, that's especially true."

Laughing, Lucas strolled off, leaving Nick grinding his teeth and Julianna staring curiously. Nick understood that Lucas hadn't been talking about their friendship. His dig had been a reference to Maggie and the fact that they hadn't gone far at all.

Where in tarnation was the woman?

Julianna had slipped her arm in his and was hauling him toward the food table when Nick finally spotted the object of his frustration.

She sat alone at one of the dozen candlelit tables placed on the lawn. Smiling at his good fortune, he quickly filled his plate and was already halfway to the table when MaryAnne Johnson and Stephanie Roberts intercepted him.

So much for his good fortune.

"Nick, honey, where you been hiding?" Stephanie drawled sweetly, a glass of white wine in one hand while she twirled a lock of coffee-colored hair with the other. "Me and MaryAnne have been looking all over for you."

"Now why would I hide from two beautiful ladies?" Nick said easily, while he glanced over MaryAnne's bleached-blond bubble-do and watched Brett Rivers, a local cattleman, sit beside Maggie. Damn. Brett was divorced and looking, Nick knew.

MaryAnne and Stephanie were always looking, too, Nick reasoned as he glanced back at the women. Even when they were married, they'd been looking. He felt like a louse to sic these two vampires on a nice guy like Brett, but all was fair. "Why don't we all go sit right over here?"

MaryAnne and Stephanie followed like hungry puppy dogs, but before they made it to the table, Nick watched Kirk Jensen slide onto the open chair on Maggie's left. Damn. Damn. Kirk was smooth as molasses when it came to the ladies.

Okay, still no problem. Three women, three men. Nick just had to maneuver the right man to the right woman. MaryAnne for Kirk, he decided. Stephanie for Brett.

And of course, Maggie for him.

Easy.

Maggie glanced up when Nick scooted into a chair across from her, the blonde on his left and the brunette on his right. She frowned at him. He grinned back broadly. "Hey, Brett, Kirk, how's it going? Hey, Maggie, look who I found. You graduated with MaryAnne and Stephanie, didn't you? Why don't we trade places so you three ladies can talk over old times and we menfolk shoot the bull."

While there was a smile on her lips, she lasered a look at him that could have burned a six-inch hole through steel. "Maybe later, Nick. Brett and Kirk and I were discussing the impact of the dam going in over at Silver Creek. I'm sure MaryAnne and Stephanie would be happy to—" she arched one delicate brow "—'shoot the bull' with you."

In fact, thought Maggie irritably, from the looks the two women were giving Nick, they'd be happy to do just about anything with him. MaryAnne's tight red dress all but had a neon sign pointing to her cleavage, while Stephanie's more tasteful turquoise dress barely covered her rather plump behind.

She forced herself to listen to Kirk explain the concern the community had regarding the effect of the dam on the local wildlife, but she found herself pulled away at MaryAnne's nails-on-the-chalkboard giggling.

She'd been having a relatively relaxed evening until Nick had shown up with the bimbos. It was bad enough to know that he found women like MaryAnne and Stephanie attractive, but to have to sit here and watch them fawn over him, to listen to them giggle and squirm beside him, was just too much. And if Stephanie said "Nick, honey," one more time, Maggie decided she would scream.

"...take a drive over to the lake one of these days and I can show you," Kirk was saying, and Maggie jerked her attention back to him. Oh, dear, had he just offered to take her somewhere?

"Why don't we *all* go?" Stephanie squeaked. "We could do that, couldn't we, Kirk?"

Kirk had obviously intended a more intimate outing, but nice guy that he was, he simply cleared his throat and smiled. "Uh, sure, I guess we could do that."

Maggie wasn't sure whether to be relieved or annoyed, but when Nick grinned at her, she decided on the latter. She frowned at him, but he simply grinned wider.

"Oh, Nick, honey." The brunette nudged Nick's arm with her own. "Won't that be fun?"

That did it. Maggie rose gracefully, smiled at Kirk and Brett. "Excuse me, I promised Mr. Winters this dance."

Without so much as a backward glance, she moved toward the dance floor, dissolved into the crowd, then emerged on the other side and followed wooden steps leading into a grove of trees. Soft lights illuminated the path that ended at a small gazebo overlooking the creek.

At least it was quiet here, except for the distant croaking of frogs from the rushing water below. She leaned against the railing, drew in a deep breath of evening air to calm herself.

Who was she kidding, anyway? She'd only been fooling herself to think that she could handle being around Nick, that she could keep a cool distance between them. There was nothing cool between them.

Hot was what she felt whenever he came close to her.
Hot and dizzy.

The sound of footsteps on the gazebo stairs made
her heart skip. She straightened, then turned slowly.

And was profoundly disappointed.

Seven

Roger Gerckee.

Maggie stared at the bully from her childhood. He leaned casually against a gazebo column, a drink of whisky in one hand and a cigarette in the other. She struggled not to roll her eyes at his ridiculous attempt to appear debonair.

Some women might think him handsome, she supposed. With his sandy-blond hair, dark blue eyes and Ivy League style, he had a look that attracted a certain type of woman. The same type of woman who probably liked cartoons on Saturday mornings.

"Hello, Roger."

Her greeting held more sigh than sincerity. She pushed away from the railing, intending to move past him, but he stood at the entrance of the gazebo, blocking her way.

"It really *is* you, isn't it?" he said, his voice slightly

slurred from the whisky. "When I asked George Moody who that gorgeous woman was, and he told me it was Margaret Smith, I said no way."

"Did you now?" She ground her teeth together. "Imagine that."

"So, I thought I better come take a look for myself." His gaze dropped to her breasts, then lifted back to her face with a grin. "And now here we are, just the two of us."

Maggie pressed her lips tightly together. "Weren't you here with a date?" she asked, praying the woman she'd seen him with earlier would show up.

"Doesn't mean I can't say hello to an old friend, does it? We could just sit here awhile and...talk."

Some people never change, she thought with disgust. Roger Gerckee was as pathetic an adult as he was a teenager.

He flicked his cigarette carelessly over the gazebo railing and if Maggie hadn't watched it drop down safely into the creek below, she would have pinched his nose and dragged him down there to pick it up. She thought about pinching his nose, anyway. Not just for the cigarette, but for the time he'd stolen her sandwich. She still owed him for that one.

It would be so easy. She was a black belt—only first-level—but taking old Roger down would be a piece of cake. A sweet piece of cake, she thought, then remembered that forgiveness and turning the other cheek had been part of her training, as well. And in truth, as pathetic as Roger was, he was also harmless.

Still, her hands twitched, and she folded them tightly behind her. "Nice chatting with you, Roger, but I have to run. I promised a dance to Ralph Winters."

She attempted to move around him, but he didn't

budge. "Ralph can wait." He took her arm. "Let's you and me dance."

"Let's not."

He held on to her arm when she tugged. A simple flip, she decided. Nothing that would break anything. She readied herself for the maneuver, but decided to give him one more chance. "Let go of me, Roger. Now."

"You heard the lady, Gerckee." Nick stepped out of the shadows into the soft glow of the gazebo lights, his narrowed, hard gaze aimed like a missile at Roger. "Let go of her. Now."

"Hey, Nick." Roger snatched his hand away. "What's up? Maggie and I were just talking."

"Your date was looking for you." Without taking his eyes off Roger, Nick strolled up the gazebo steps. "I think she wanted to say goodnight. She was putting her coat on, but you might catch her before she leaves."

Roger's head snapped up. His date leaving before him had obviously not been part of his plan. "Oh, yeah. Right. I guess I better do that. Well, ah, see you around, Nick. Maggie."

"Not if I see you first," Maggie muttered when Roger scurried away. She glanced back at Nick, but he was still frowning after Roger. She still wasn't certain whether she was relieved that Nick had shown up, or disappointed. The idea of tossing Roger on his butt had held a certain primitive pleasure.

And yet, Nick coming to her rescue held a certain primitive pleasure, as well, though one of an entirely different nature.

Turning, she leaned her back against the rail and

smiled. "I believe this is the part where I'm supposed to bat my eyes and cry. 'My hero!'"

Nick scowled at her. Plainly, he was not in a teasing mood. "I should have thrown that jerk over the railing."

"That would have been littering." Staring into the shadows, she smiled wistfully. "Though I do seem to recall an incident with Roger and a trash can when I was thirteen."

"One of my fondest memories," he said dryly, then leaned against the railing beside her.

"Mine, too." Sounds drifted up from the party—people laughing, a slow, lost-love number from the band. "Do you remember why you dumped him in that trash can?"

"Knowing Roger, it could be any one of a hundred reasons."

"You did it because of me."

He lifted his head, stared at her. "Yeah?"

"Yeah. We were in the lunch court. Roger had been making fun of me, then he grabbed my sandwich and threw it away. That's when you dumped him in the trash can."

Nick frowned at the memory. "I'd wanted to punch his lights out, but Lucas and Ian talked me out of it." He touched her cheek, slid his finger lightly over her jaw. "So that was you, was it?"

She nodded slowly, mesmerized by the gentle touch of his fingertip on her skin. "I remember every detail, even what you were wearing. White T-shirt, faded blue jeans and a worn, black leather jacket. The look in your eyes was fierce, a little frightening, but wonderfully exciting at the same time."

She realized he was looking at her like that right

now, and she felt the same way she had fifteen years ago. Frightened, but wonderfully excited. Her skin tingled from his touch. That's all it took from him, just a simple touch and he made her feel alive, made her want things she could never have.

With a sigh, she leaned into him, lifted her face so she could look into his eyes. "No one had ever been a champion to quiet, plain little Maggie Smith. When the other kids cheered, for just that one moment I felt like a princess who'd been rescued by the black knight." She smiled softly. "You were my hero, Nick Santos."

His eyes turned dark as the shadows surrounding them, and he stared at her with an intensity that made her shiver. "Is that what the connection is with us, Maggie?" he asked quietly. "Is that why I feel as if there's something between us, something that I should be remembering, but can't quite pull out of the cobwebs?"

She went still at his words, realized that she'd said too much, that she'd let herself get too close, not just physically, but emotionally. A dangerous, foolish thing to do. There was a connection far beyond that day, and she could never let him know what it was.

She straightened and pushed herself away from the railing, from his touch. Where her skin had burned only a moment before, she now felt cold and frightened.

"There's no connection between us, Nick," she said evenly. "Only that we lived in the same town and went to the same schools. I had a childish infatuation with you, just like half the other girls in school did, that's all."

She rubbed at the chill that had settled into her arms, felt suddenly tired, though it was still early. She had to make him understand that nothing was going to happen between them, that they could never be lovers.

"That foolish little Maggie doesn't exist anymore." Her voice was steady, firm. "She's all grown-up now. She lives in the real world, where ordinary people build their relationships on hard work and a serious commitment to each other, not childhood fantasies or one-night stands."

He straightened, his mouth set in a firm, hard line as he stared down at her. It was several long moments before he finally spoke. "I need to take you home now, Maggie," he said evenly.

Of course he would want to take her home, she thought. Now that he'd finally gotten it through his head that she wasn't going to go to bed with him, he'd want to get rid of her as quickly as possible. Why wouldn't he, when there were plenty of women more than ready to accommodate him? The night was young, he could dump her and still find a woman willing to have a private party with him. She told herself that it was for the best, that this was the way it had to be, but that didn't ease the pain in her heart one little bit.

"You go on, Nick." She forced her voice to be light. "I'll find a ride home."

"I brought you here." He took her elbow, was already moving her back toward the party. "I'll take you home."

"But—"

"Don't argue with me, Maggie. Just get your coat." They bumped into several guests as he dragged her across the back lawn.

"I haven't even said goodbye to Lucas or Julianna," she protested, struggling to keep up with his long strides.

"I'll call them tomorrow." They were inside the house now and he nearly pushed her down the hallway toward the bedroom being used as a coatroom. "I'll be waiting at the truck."

She opened her mouth to argue, but he'd already turned and walked away before she could get the words out. Of all the nerve! Who did he think he was!

Nick Santos was just a little too full of himself, she decided, and intended to tell him so. What right did he have to get angry because she wouldn't go to bed with him?

The *arrogance*. She snatched her coat from the bed and yanked it on. The *audacity*. She found her purse and snapped it onto her shoulder.

She was almost to the door when Roger stepped into the bedroom and closed the door behind him. Oh, God, she groaned inwardly. *Not now.*

"Hello, again." He closed the door behind him. "I noticed Nick just left. I thought maybe we could finish our discussion."

"We weren't having a discussion. Now if you'll excuse me, I'd like to pass."

"We've got a lot to catch up on, Maggie. It's been a long time."

"Not long enough, Gerckee."

If he hadn't reached for her arm when she tried to move past him, and if she hadn't felt so agitated, she might have waited a moment to react. But the fact was he *did* grab her arm, and she was very, *very* agitated.

So in one smooth, easy move, she flipped him onto his back.

Eyes wide, jaw slack, Roger lay perfectly still on the floor. She knelt beside him and sighed. "Don't ever touch me again, got that?"

He nodded mutely.

"Good night, Roger,"

She stood, straightened her coat and purse and slipped out of the bedroom. Nick already had his truck running and he stood beside the open driver door, his face tight with impatience. "What took you so long?"

"I had to give a hand to someone," she said dryly, then squeaked when he took hold of her by the waist and hefted her none too gently up into the truck. Frowning, she scooted across the seat and settled back while he slammed the truck into gear and tore off, spinning gravel with his back wheels.

The air in the truck cab crackled with the heat of their tension. He obviously was in no mood for idle chitchat, and she decided she'd wait until they got to her house to give him a piece of her mind.

But instead of turning left at Woodrow Street, the direction he should have taken, he turned right.

"You missed the street," she said tightly.

"Nope."

"What do you mean, 'nope'? You know perfectly well that you have to take Woodrow to get to my parents' house."

He turned sharply into the parking lot of his shop. "Of course I know that."

"You said you were taking me home, Nick."

"I am taking you home." He got out of the truck, came around and opened her door. "*My* home."

She opened her mouth to argue, but when he reached in and lifted her in his arms, she forgot what she wanted to say. He carried her to the entrance of his shop, slid the key into the lock and kicked the door open. When he closed the door again, she finally found her voice.

"Nick Santos, put me down right now."

"Nope." A light from a workbench lamp lit the inside of the shop. He carried her into the office, through the door of his living quarters, flipped on the wall light switch, then deposited her into an overstuffed chair beside a small bookcase.

When she started to jump up, he pointed a finger at her. "Sit. You are going to listen to me, Margaret Smith Hamilton, and listen close, because what I'm about to say I've never said to any woman before and I will not repeat it."

Her anger warred with her curiosity, but curiosity won. Folding her arms, she eased back into the chair and glared at him.

"I've never felt the need to explain myself to anyone," he said irritably, pacing the small confines of his combination bedroom, kitchen and living area. "What I do, what I've done is nobody's business but my own."

"Nick—"

He paused mid-stride and pointed his index finger sharply at her. She pressed her lips tightly together.

"I like women." He stomped to the tiny kitchen, turned and faced her, hands on his hips. "I certainly won't apologize for that."

"I'm not asking—"

"Shut up and listen. I like women, I've dated a lot of them, but that doesn't mean I've slept with every one of them. In spite of what you seem to think of me, I've actually slept with very few of them, and not one of them was a 'one-night stand,' as you seem to be so fond of accusing me. Every woman I've been with meant something to me. I cared about them."

He stared at her, his face rigid, his eyes narrowed

and hard. "I care about you, Maggie. From that first moment I picked you out of that pile of green bean cans, I felt something for you. I won't deny it's partly physical, nor will I apologize because I want to take you to bed. At least I'm honest about that, which is a hell of a lot more than you're being with me."

Her heart missed a beat. "What do you mean?"

"You know exactly what I mean. You're just as attracted to me as I am to you. You don't want to be just *friends* with me any more than I do with you. We both want a hell of a lot more than that, but you haven't got the guts to admit it." He dragged his hands through his hair in frustration. "Who hurt you so bad that you're afraid to let yourself live, to let yourself feel? Was it your ex-husband?"

You, she wanted to blurt out, to let loose the tension coiled inside her. But even if she could, even if she did, he would never believe her. He would only hate her.

She closed her eyes against the threatening tears. "It was a long time ago, Nick, before I was married. I was young...I got swept up in the moment...but it wasn't...it was only—"

She couldn't bring herself to say it. Couldn't bear to make the most wonderful night of her life sound cheap or sleazy. She felt Nick's hands on her arms and opened her eyes, hating the tear that slid down her cheek.

"Oh, geez, Maggie." He knelt in front of her, took her hands gently in his. "Is that what you're trying to say? That you had a one-night stand?"

She nodded.

He tugged her off the chair into his lap. "You can't beat yourself up over something like that. It happens."

"Not to me, not to good little Margaret Smith. I'd never done anything like that before. Or since."

She stared at her hands clasped together in her lap. "But that wasn't all," she said softly. "It was so unexpected, so…sudden, that I—"

"You what?"

"I…got pregnant."

He went still. "Drew?"

"Yes."

He sighed, then cuddled her against him and kissed her forehead. "And the man you were with, Drew's father?"

"He…wasn't around."

"The bastard."

"No," she said quickly, then more softly, "please don't ask my any more, just believe me, it wasn't like that."

As dangerous as this conversation was, Maggie knew she could tell Nick all this and there still was no way he would ever know the whole truth. She *needed* to tell him, needed him to understand, if only a little, why she'd behaved the way she had. She was certain she would regret it tomorrow, but at this moment, sitting on Nick's lap, his arms holding her tenderly, there was no tomorrow, no yesterday. No past, no future.

Only now.

She felt safe in the shelter of his arms, as if she'd come home at last. The tension that had knotted her insides shifted from fear and anger to something entirely different. The warmth of his body seeped into hers, and she felt herself softening, melting into him. His aftershave, a masculine, erotic scent, curled deep in her lungs, triggered a primal response that was impossible to ignore or deny.

And the truth was she no longer wanted to deny it. No longer wanted to ignore it. And what better way to put out a fire then to let it run wild?

She turned in his arms, cupped his cheek in her hand, then traced his lips with her fingertips. His body stiffened against hers; his eyes darkened, narrowed at the corners.

"You wanted truth," she murmured, "this is it. I want to make love with you, Nick. I want to feel your mouth on my lips, your hands on my skin." She yanked at his shirt, pulled it roughly from his jeans and slipped her hands underneath. His muscles jumped at her touch.

"And most of all," she whispered as she brushed her lips, just barely, over his, "most of all, I want to feel you inside me."

Eight

For one long, heart-stopping moment, Nick swore that he'd heard her wrong, that he'd simply imagined her asking him to make love to him. He couldn't trust himself to move, to even speak. If he did, he was certain she would vanish and he'd wake up from the dream.

But if this was a dream, it was one hell of a doozy. The woman nestled in his arms was all curves—smooth, cool silk and warm, soft velvet. Her scent was feminine, seductive and incredibly arousing. Her hands soothed over his cheeks, her eyes deepened to a smoky green as she raised her face to his.

Light as a whisper, her lips brushed his. "Kiss me, Nick. Please."

He needed no other encouragement. On a groan, he covered her mouth hungrily with his. Her arms came around his neck, and her soft breasts flattened against his chest. He groaned again, dragging her closer still while he kissed her with all the pent-up frustration from what seemed like a lifetime of wanting this, of wanting her.

"Maggie," he murmured, dragging his mouth over her smooth, silky throat, "have you any idea how crazy I am for you, how much I want you?"

Her response was a throaty, sensual sigh. She dipped her head backward, exposing more of her delicious skin, and he feasted on the sweetness, trailed hot kisses over the base of her neck, the ridge of her collarbone, down to the soft swell of her breast. He felt the quickening of her breath, the tiny gasp of delight as he nuzzled aside her suit jacket and made contact with black lace.

Every primal instinct screamed at him to take her now, hard and fast, to bury himself deeply inside her and ease the throbbing ache in his loins. But strangely, he needed more than that from Maggie, more than he'd ever needed from any woman before. And stranger yet was the feeling that somehow he'd come home, that holding her in his arms, making love to her, was as natural to him as breathing.

She squirmed in his arms, and the movement brought her firm, rounded bottom snugly against his arousal. Groaning, he stilled her restless hips with his hand, then leaned her back against the easy chair to free his other arm. Eyes heavy with desire, Maggie rolled her head backward while she ran her hands up his arms, then tugged at the collar of his jacket and pulled it down. He shrugged the garment off and tossed it, then turned his attention to the soft velvet-covered buttons of her suit jacket. Slowly, one by one, he slid each button open, keeping his gaze locked with hers until the jacket fell open.

Sheer black lace cupped her breasts. Her skin was pale in the dim light of the room, and through the delicate texture of lace, he saw the rosy outline of her hardened nipples. Heat exploded in his veins, then burst into flames.

"Do you know how beautiful you are?" he asked hoarsely, circling her narrow waist with his hands. Her skin was warm and silky, smooth as cream, and he slid his thumbs upward across her flat stomach, lightly brushed the underside of her breasts. She trembled at his touch. "Do you, Maggie Smith?"

Maggie tried to answer him, but words simply failed her. A river of liquid heat flooded her body, pooled low in her belly and between her legs. Her skin felt tight and hot, and the slow rhythm of his thumbs on her breasts left her dizzy and weak. Closing her eyes, she let her head fall back against the chair. His thumbs moved upward again, a slow, sensuous massage, and she moaned softly.

He bent over her, closed his lips over one lace-covered nipple and kneaded the sensitive skin with his teeth and lips. She gasped, then shuddered at the intense waves of pleasure rolling through her. His mouth was doing the most amazing, most glorious things to her, and she lost herself to the feelings, just as she'd lost herself to the man so many years ago.

Deftly his fingers unclasped the front hook of her bra, exposing her bare breasts. She felt the cool air mix with his warm breath, the gentle caress of his large, callused palms on her skin. She arched forward on a groan as his lips closed over one beaded nipple. His mouth was hot and wet, the pleasure so great it bordered on pain. She dragged her hands through his dark, thick hair, dug her fingers into his scalp while she pulled him still closer.

"Nick, please," she pleaded, and moved restlessly under him. "I need you."

"I need you, too, baby," he said raggedly, then gripped her hips in his hands. "I need you so bad it's killing me. But I've thought about you, about this, too long. You're mine, Maggie, all night, and I'm not going to rush one precious minute."

His words excited and tormented her at the same time. She thought she couldn't bear it, this delicious torture of his hands and lips as he moved over her. While his mouth worked its magic on her heated skin, he slid one hand down her thigh, lower, to the curve of her calf, then down to her feet, carefully removing each high heel before skimming back up her leg. His fingertips burned a trail on the sensitive flesh of her inner thigh, then slowly rolled down the lace tops of her silk stockings and removed them, as well.

Her legs were long, like satin, made for a man's hand, Nick thought possessively. *His* hand. The struggle to control his raging desire was nearly lost as he explored the arch of her foot, the smooth skin behind her knee, then higher still, up to the soft, sweet vee of her thighs. He could be blissfully lost here forever. He pushed her skirt upward, traced one finger along the thin strip of lace across her hips, then slid underneath, into the hot, moist glove of her body.

Gasping, she strained toward him on a whimper, then raked her hands through his hair and pulled his mouth roughly back to hers. He stroked her, and she matched the rhythm, opening to him as her hands slid anxiously under his shirt. She moved her palms over his bare, damp skin, skimmed her smooth fingertips through the coarse hair on his chest. Intense, hot pleasure throbbed in his blood as she murmured her approval, and when her hand moved to the buckle of his belt, his breath caught, then rushed out on a groan.

He knew his control was thread thin, and when her hands roamed lower, to the zipper of his jeans, then lightly slid over the hard length of his arousal, he knew he couldn't wait any longer.

His breathing was harsh and deep as he moved away from her, then scooped her up in his arms and carried her to the bed. Her arms wound around his neck, her lips pressing urgent kisses to the base of his throat. They fell together on the bed and rolled in a tangle of arms and legs, struggling to remove clothing between heated kisses and roaming hands. Even as he reached into the bedside table for the necessary precaution, he kept his gaze locked with hers. Her skin was flushed, translucent in the soft light; her eyes were heavy with desire.

Desire for him, he realized, and pulled her beneath him with a fierce need to possess he'd never experienced before.

"Nick." She reached for him, pleading, and the sound of his name on her lips inflamed his already-burning senses.

His control snapped and he moved over her, between her legs, watching her while he slid into the tight, slick glove of her body. She arched upward to take him more deeply and he groaned, a mixture of pain and pleasure and amazement at the intensity of sensations pounding his insides. The need to thrust even deeper, even harder, overwhelmed him, but with a will born of iron, he stilled her writhing hips, wanting this moment, this joining, to last as long as possible.

He braced his arms over her, lowered his face slowly to hers. His body coiled with need, sweat beaded his forehead, but he took his time, brushed his mouth over hers and tasted the passion on her lips. Her arms wound tightly around his neck, dragged him closer, and she kissed him with a desperation that took his breath away. He felt the longing in her surrender, the need, but there was something more, something he couldn't quite recognize. But when she slid her long, silky legs over his and tightened her body around him, he could no longer think.

He began to move, slowly at first, eased himself deeply inside her, felt her tremble as she received him, heard her gasp of pleasure as she moved with him. He rolled his hips again and she dug her fingernails into his back on a sharp intake of breath. When she sobbed his name he could hold back no longer. The fever exploded inside him, and his blood burst into flame. He drove himself into her, and she met him with each wild thrust. The flames rose higher, hotter, consuming them both with the need for each other, with the need for completion.

He felt the shudders rip through her body, then let himself go with her.

She couldn't move. Couldn't think. She felt as if she were floating in a dark, quiet tunnel. As if she'd been born, as if she'd died. And she was finally at peace with the demon that had plagued her for five years.

Nick brushed his lips against hers, then gathered her in his arms and rolled them both to their sides. She rubbed her cheek against the solid, damp wall of his chest, loving the sound of his rapid, heavy heartbeat.

Loving him.

What a fool she'd been to think she could resist Nick, that she could deny her feelings, both physical and emotional. No man had ever made her feel this way before, made her feel so completely alive. No man ever would again.

She knew that she'd regret this night, part of her already did. But she could never regret loving him any more than she could regret Drew. Through Drew a part of Nick would always be with her.

"You okay?" he murmured, kissing the top of her head.

The best answer she could muster resembled something close to a purr.

He laughed softly. "I'll take that as a yes."

Unable to help herself, she ran one hand over his steellike biceps, trailed her fingertips over his hip, then smoothed her palm over his muscular thigh. The dark, rough hair tickled her fingers, accentuated masculine against feminine. He sucked in a sharp breath at her touch, tightened his hand on her back.

Her fingers stilled at the edge of a large, jagged scar that ran from his lower thigh, over his knee, and halfway down his left leg. Two smaller, faded scars zigzagged at his calf. Frowning, she glanced up at him.

"That was the day I found out I couldn't fly," he said lightly, but his eyes were somber when he looked down.

"The Colorado accident?"

He nodded, pulled her with him as he rolled to his back. "I read somewhere that scars are supposed to be sexy. What do you think?"

She merely frowned at him. As if the man needed any help with sex appeal. If he had any more, he'd have to register himself as a lethal weapon. Supporting her head in her hand while she rested one elbow lightly on his chest, she ran the length of the scar with her fingertip. He jumped when she traced one of the pale, slender lines across his calf.

"This one looks older," she said, pleased that even though they'd just made love, she was still able to evoke a physical response from him. And she was certainly experiencing her own reaction, as well. Touching him like this, so intimately, so tenderly, was playing havoc not only with her body, but with her heart, too.

"That one I owe to Ian." Enjoying the sensual touch of her fingertip, Nick closed his eyes and tucked one hand behind his head.

"Ian?" She followed the scar upward, to the inside of his leg. He drew in a slow, deep breath.

"We were fifteen, riding double on my first scooter. He leaned the wrong way around a curve and we crashed. One of the wheel spokes popped, ripped through my jeans, then into my leg. It was the only time I ever hit him that he didn't hit me back."

She paused. "You hit him?"

"Of course I hit him," Nick said with a puff of indignation. "He crashed my scooter. He expected me to hit him. It was a matter of honor." He smiled wickedly and wiggled his eyebrows. "Next time I see him, though, I'm definitely going to thank him."

"You wouldn't." She started to sit, but with a laugh, Nick took hold of her wrists and pulled her on top of him.

"Just kidding." When he saw the look of panic in her eyes, though, he narrowed his eyes. "You don't have a thing for Ian, do you? I would definitely have to punch him if you do."

She nearly laughed at the absurdity. "No, Nick, I

don't have 'a thing' for Ian, and you most certainly don't have to punch him. Besides, when would you have the opportunity? You said yourself how difficult he was to get hold of.''

"Sometimes, yes, sometimes no," he answered in that same cryptic tone he used every time Ian's name was mentioned. When he trailed his fingertips down her neck, then over her shoulder, she shivered.

"Are you trying to distract me?" She closed her eyes as he dipped into the valley between her breasts, then moved upward again.

"Maybe I don't feel like hearing you talk about another man at this moment.'' He discovered a sensitive spot at the base of her neck and using his mouth and tongue, he concentrated his efforts on that one exquisite spot.

She gasped when his teeth nipped her skin. "All right, then." She shivered at the pleasure skipping through her body right to her toes. "Let's talk about you.''

"My favorite subject," he murmured, still exploring the curve of her neck with his mouth.

She laughed softly, then drew in a slow, deep breath as his hands roamed down her back. "Tell me why you left Wolf River and never came back until now."

He laid his head back on a pillow and looked up at her. "You know the saying, 'So many racetracks, so little time'? The rush of adrenaline was as seductive as it was addictive, and I was hooked. I was also pretty damn good," he said with a cocky grin.

"You were the best." The feel of his long, hard body under hers, the slide of his work-roughened hands over her bottom, made her ache for him again. Ever so slightly, she pressed her hips against his, delighted at the desire that darkened his eyes. "But twelve years is a long time," she said quietly, forcing her mind to concentrate, when her body threatened to rebel. "You never came back, not even once."

He shrugged. "There was nothing for me here. Lucas and Ian were gone, my stepfather drank himself into Wolf River cemetery, and I was too focused on my career to look back. Racing was the only thing I'd ever been really good at, the only thing I'd ever wanted."

"And now?" she asked softly. "What is it you want now, Nick?"

A long, silent moment passed between them as he stared up at her. She shivered at the intensity in his dark eyes, wished she could take her question back. A question she should never have asked. Without warning, he flipped her onto her back and raised her arms over her head.

"I want you, Maggie," he said roughly. "I want you."

Excitement raced through her blood. "Nick, I have to go," she whispered raggedly, but even she heard the weakness in her voice.

"Not a chance." He shook his head slowly. "Like I told you, sweetheart, you're all mine for the night and I'm not letting you go."

His mouth dropped down to cover hers, and she opened to him, arched upward, felt herself melt into him as he kissed her hard and deep.

She shuddered at his touch, at his words, felt the heat rush through her veins as his mouth closed over hers again. One night, she told herself and gave herself up to the kiss. One wonderful night.

He cupped her breasts, rubbed the hardened peaks

with his thumbs, and she moved against him, already needing him inside her again. Moaning, she clung to him, ran her hands over his broad chest and flat belly. His breathing grew ragged and harsh, and the sound he made was low and guttural. His kiss turned desperate, and he plundered her mouth, her senses, left her gasping and wild with need.

His eyes were nearly black, narrowed and glinting with desire as he knelt between her legs and stared down at her. Her heart pounded furiously, her breathing grew shallow as she held his gaze. His hands moved up her thighs, and with his palm he caressed the aching, swollen mound between her legs. She bit her bottom lip on a whimper and rolled her hips, torn between the desire to curse him or beg him to take her.

He smiled wickedly at her response. "Do you still have to go?"

"You don't play fair, Nick Santos," she whispered, reaching for him as he slowly lowered his body over hers.

"All's fair," he murmured and slid into her body.

In love and war, she finished silently, not certain which one they were dealing with here. But when he moved inside her, when he grew harder and bigger, she couldn't think at all anymore. She could only feel. She wrapped her arms around his neck, her legs around his waist, and let herself go with the exquisite feeling. Damp skin against damp skin, the rough brush of his chest hair against her breasts, his mouth, insistent and demanding, on hers.

Her back arched with the first shuddering convulsion, and she heard his harsh groan in response as he followed her. Pleasure slammed through her, again and again, until she fell back, shattered yet complete.

He eased away from her, then cradled her gently in his arms. With a sigh she settled against him, and the words he'd said to her earlier came rushing at her like a cold burst of wind.

I care about you, Maggie.

Did he? she wondered. Did he really? His words thrilled her.

But even if he did, she thought miserably, nothing could come of this, of them. There was no way to go back now. Even if she wanted to tell him everything, how could she? He'd hate her, maybe even hate Drew, because he was part of the lie. And there was no way forward, because she couldn't be a part of his life, not with a lie between them, a lie that would only destroy any chance for happiness they might have.

No, she knew she would have only this night, this one wonderful night and that night almost five years ago. It would have to be enough, she thought. The ache he stirred in her body was nothing compared to the ache he stirred in her heart.

And with that ache came the crush of reality. She closed her eyes against the burn of tears. She would regret this night, she knew, as much as she would cherish it.

At 1:00 a.m. the porch light was on when Nick pulled up in front of Maggie's parents' house. The dormer windows were pitch-black, as were all the windows in all the houses on the street.

Maggie had been quiet on the drive back, and he knew that she was already pulling away from him. He just didn't understand why.

There was too much about this woman that he didn't understand. Too damn much.

"Well," she said awkwardly, "I really do have to get in. I wouldn't want my parents to—"

"Just sit with me a minute." He took her arm and pulled her across the seat until their sides were touching.

He felt the tension in her body, the hesitation. But then she nodded and relaxed a bit. They sat there, neither one of them speaking, and the stillness of the early morning closed around them like a soft glove. Not once in his entire life had he ever remembered a feeling of such utter content, of such peace.

He looked out the window of his truck at the clean sidewalks, the carefully mowed lawns, the neat flower beds and pruned trees. He'd always envied people like these. Fathers who took their sons to Little League games, mothers who fussed over birthdays, family picnics and Easter egg hunts. It had always felt like a private club that only the privileged could join.

It still felt that way, only now he felt a sense of longing, a sense that he'd missed something important. Something that everyone else but him had admission to. Something that would always be just out of his reach.

Only Lucas and Ian understood that feeling, though not one of them would have admitted it. They'd spent too much time growing up trying to be tough, to prove to everyone they didn't give a damn. He was still trying to prove that, not only to everyone else, but himself, as well.

And now Lucas had Julianna, and Ian was God knew where.

He turned to Maggie, pulled her against him and kissed her with a need that surprised him. Her hands splayed on his chest, her fingers moved restlessly, and he ached for her again.

He broke the kiss suddenly, watched her green eyes open slowly and saw the desire there, as well. "This wasn't a one-night stand, Maggie," he said roughly. "I'll be back. Not only tomorrow, but the day after that and the day after that, too. You can count on it."

"Nick." She stared over his shoulder into the darkness. "I'm leaving in three weeks."

We'll see about that, he thought fiercely. "Then we have three weeks. You and me and Drew. And starting tomorrow, I mean today—" he glanced at his watch "—in exactly nine hours, I'm picking you both up for a picnic."

She started to shake her head, but he dragged her against him and kissed her again. He felt her resistance melt, then heard her sigh of surrender.

They steamed the windows before he finally walked her to the front door. And long after their last long, smoldering kiss at the door, long after she'd walked inside and turned off the porch light, he sat in his truck and watched, wondering what it was about Maggie Smith that had a hold of him and wouldn't let go.

Nine

A jazz band was performing in the park the following afternoon, filling the warm air with a mixture of Dixieland and blues. A breeze carried the scent of grilling hot dogs and hamburgers and gently shook the leaves of the cottonwood and fir trees that provided shade for dozens of blankets and quilts spread over the soft, green grass. Teenagers in oversize T-shirts and baggy shorts shot hoops on a nearby basketball court, while the smaller children played on swings and slides in a large, sand-covered area.

A typical day at the park, Maggie thought, except that she and Drew happened to be here with Nick Santos. And there was absolutely nothing typical about that.

With a sigh she slipped off her leather sandals, tucked her long, floral-print skirt around her knees and knelt on the blanket Nick had spread out in the shade of a tall cottonwood. Drew had begged Nick to push him on the swings, and she'd waved them off to play while she unpacked the army-size basket of food her mother had insisted on making: tuna salad on wheat bread, ham and cheese on fresh rolls, three kinds of salad, baked beans, spiced chicken wings, fresh-baked chocolate chip cookies, pecan tarts and what seemed like four gallons of lemonade. There was enough food in their basket to feed a small country and still have leftovers.

She knew what her mother was up to. She'd had that look in her eyes since that first day Nick had shown up. That you've-been-single-too-long look that Maggie knew only too well. But she'd been down that road, for all the wrong reasons. She was older now, though not necessarily wiser, she thought, as she looked over at Nick, watched him playing with her son. Their son.

Not wise at all.

But logic and reason had been bound and tied by her heart. She cursed her own weakness, but she simply couldn't resist spending these few precious hours with Nick, or even the next few days. The pain of leaving again would be a small price to pay for the happiness.

But what would be the price to pay if by some wild, crazy happening, Nick remembered that night five years ago, remembered even one little thing that might somehow tie back to her? What if even one person were to put a thought in his head that Drew might be his son?

No. She shook off the dread that snaked through her, even forced a laugh at the absurdity. Impossible. He would never connect her back to that night in the hotel. She doubted he remembered that night at all. She was safe. And as long as she was safe, Drew was safe.

Maggie felt her heart skip as she watched Nick. He looked handsome as the devil today in a black Stetson and black T-shirt, and she knew that every female within sight was drooling over that long, powerful body wrapped in snug denim and smooth cotton. She knew she was. Every time he pushed Drew, Nick's muscles bunched and rippled under his T-shirt. She couldn't take her eyes off him, couldn't believe that only last night, for a few hours, he'd actually been hers.

Head thrown back, Drew shrieked with laughter when Nick pushed him higher. She knew what that felt like, that wild, high-in-the-sky feeling of ecstasy. All it took was a simple look, a simple touch from Nick and she was soaring, her feet off the ground and her head in the clouds.

Watching the two of them, the two people she loved more than life itself, made her chest swell. She wanted to remember every minute they were together, every sound, every sight, every smell. Later, when she and Drew were back in New York, when the nights were long, her bed cold and lonely, she would recall every precious moment.

And last night, she thought with a shiver of pleasure, last night she would always remember. Every whisper, every kiss, every brush of his hand. And this time when they'd made love, it had been her name on Nick's lips, not another woman's. Last night he'd known exactly who he was making love to. He'd wanted *her*, Maggie Smith. And *that* she would hold close for the rest of her life.

Drew called to her, and she waved. Nick winked at her, and she felt her heart stop, then start to race. The look in his eyes was hungry, and she knew it was for more than food. She was feeling exactly the same way.

She knew that they'd make love again, and she felt a mixture of excitement and misery at that realization. He was everything she wanted and everything she could never have.

The food was laid out when Drew came running back from the swings. He circled the large, green-plaid blanket Maggie had spread out, bounced up, then landed with a smack on his bottom.

"Did you see me, Mom?" He reached for a cookie. "Did you see how high I went?"

She snatched the cookie from him and handed him a wet cloth to wipe his hands. "You went so high all the birds in the trees scattered," she teased.

Nick plopped down on the blanket beside her, wrapped an arm around her shoulders, and kissed her straight on the lips before she could protest. It wasn't a passionate kiss, but it wasn't a simple one, either. It was possessive, lingering, with a quick touch of tongues. Her gaze flew to her son, whose big, dark brown eyes had widened. He'd been too little to remember Richard, and he'd never seen a man kiss her before. Her cheeks flushed, partly from embarrassment, partly from the thrill of Nick's lips on hers.

"You kissed my mom," Drew said to Nick in astonishment. "How come?"

"'Cause I like her a whole bunch." Nick kept his arm around her. "Is that okay?"

Drew thought about that for a moment, then gave a small shrug of his shoulders. "It's okay with me, if it's okay with her."

Maggie's cheeks flushed hotter when both Nick and Drew looked at her. What could she possibly say? She didn't want her son to start thinking that Nick was anything more than a friend, but at the same time she didn't want him to think she kissed "friends" full on the mouth all the time, either.

"Uh, sure. It's okay, sweetie," was all she could manage, hoping that her son wouldn't pursue the matter.

Distracted by a dog barking, Drew glanced away. "Hey, that's Joshua from my school." He waved at a freckled blond boy throwing a ball to a golden retriever. The boy waved back, then called for Drew to come play ball with him. Drew looked hopefully at his mother, and when she nodded, he shouted to his friend, then grabbed two cookies before she could stop him and took off like a bullet.

Drew had the long, sure stride of an athlete, Nick thought as he watched the boy run. He wondered briefly if Drew's father had been an athlete, if maybe the man Maggie had been with had been a sports figure she'd met through her job on the paper, maybe someone she'd had to interview. His jaw clenched at the thought of that guy, the son of a bitch who'd left her alone and pregnant. Part of him wished he knew who the bastard was. He had enough friends in the sports world to make the guy's life a living hell.

But part of him didn't want to know, didn't even want to think about her being with that guy. Being with any other guy.

He forced his irritation away and pulled her closer, kissed her again, only this time longer and with less restraint than the first time, when little eyes had been on them. He felt her sway toward him, answer him with a soft whimper deep in her throat as she kissed him back.

"Nick." She broke the kiss suddenly. "Please."

He leaned close, breathed in the light scent of her

floral perfume as he whispered, "When you said please last night, it meant *more*."

She kept her hand firmly on his chest to hold him away, and when he covered her fingers with his, he felt the wild beating of her pulse. The heat that had been on her cheeks before spread over her face and down her neck. "You know what I mean. We can't do that here, now."

He glanced around at the couples walking hand in hand, the families enjoying their picnics, at the people dancing by the band, then looked back at her. "Why not?"

She hesitated, then glanced at her son. "I don't want Drew to be confused about us. He might not... understand."

"I don't understand, and I'm more than a little confused about us." He rubbed his thumbs over the backs of her smooth, soft hands, remembered what those hands felt like on his skin last night, and grew instantly hard. "Why don't you explain it to me?"

She looked away, stared down at his hands covering hers. "I told you, I'm leaving in three weeks. It might be difficult for Drew if he became too...attached."

"What about you, Maggie?" he whispered. "Would it be difficult for you if you became attached?"

Her gaze was steady as she met his. "We're adults, Nick. We understand how to deal with and control our feelings."

She was wrong there. He had no idea how to deal with these feelings she stirred in him, and he sure as hell had no control. He wanted her, more than he'd ever wanted any other woman. But it wasn't just sex, it was more. Much more. He told himself that in three weeks he'd feel different. That she'd leave and he would be fine. His life would go back to normal, status quo, and he'd settle back into his comfortable bachelor routine.

But that was in three weeks. A lifetime. Right now he simply couldn't let it go. Couldn't let her go.

"All right, then. We'll do it your way. When Drew's around I'll be good." He brushed an auburn curl from her cheek and lowered his lips within a whisper of hers. "But when he's not around, I suggest you watch out, 'cause I intend to be bad." His voice deepened and he nipped softly at her bottom lip. "Very bad."

He watched her eyes turn smoky-green, saw her lips softly part, then felt her tremble under his hands. She leaned toward him, let her eyes slowly close.

He dropped his hands away, then stood. Maggie swayed, opened her eyes and blinked.

"I'm going to go play a little football with the boys," he said, frustrated as well as pleased by her response to his near kiss. "You just think about what I said."

Think about what he said? Maggie watched Nick swagger away, torn between cursing him or making him come back and kiss her. She could *feel* what he said, straight down to her curled toes. Her skin felt tight; her breasts tingled. She could barely breathe.

She'd *think* about it, all right, she thought, her body aching for him. His mouth, his hands, his lips. On her. Everywhere, all at once.

"Maggie!"

Startled out of her fantasy, Maggie looked up at Julianna. Her wide-brimmed straw hat shaded her face and her loose denim dress draped softly over her rounded stomach.

"Julianna." Maggie's voice cracked, and she had to clear her throat. "Hi."

"Hi, yourself." She turned, waved a hand at Lucas, who was loaded down with a folding chair, picnic basket, blanket and plastic cooler. He lifted his chin in a nod and made his way toward them. "Mind if we join you?"

"I'd love it." Especially if it kept her mind off Nick, she thought. When Lucas staggered up, she stood and took the blanket and cooler from him.

"Hey, beautiful." Lucas gave her a peck on the cheek, which delighted and made her blush at the same time. "I saw his truck, but couldn't believe there was a woman alive who could get Nick Santos out on a Sunday-afternoon picnic. That boy's reputation is ruined for good."

"Don't listen to him, Maggie." Julianna eased down into the chair Lucas unfolded for her. "Lucas is just jealous because his own bad-boy reputation was ruined when he got married, and now he's going to be a daddy in four weeks, too. He can't stand it that Nick and Ian are still free as birds."

"Not true, my love." Lucas bent and kissed his wife, then gently ran a hand over her stomach. "With you, I'll take the ball and chain over wings any day."

Frowning, she pushed him away, but love and pleasure shone in her soft-blue eyes. "Go play, dear. Nick's waving at you."

He gave her a swift smack on the lips and took off at a dead run. To the delight of Drew and his friend, Lucas caught Nick and tackled him soundly. Both men went down hard, arms and legs flying.

Julianna shook her head at their nonsense. "Boys. Can't live with 'em, can't live without 'em."

How true it was, Maggie thought with a sigh. "Your party was wonderful last night, Julianna. Thank you for inviting me."

"You and Nick left early." Julianna tipped her hat up. "Seemed that you were in a bit of a hurry, too."

Did she know? Maggie worried. Was it that obvious that she and Nick had slept together? "I...well, we—"

Julianna laughed and patted Maggie's arm. "Don't worry, Mag. Your secret's safe with me, though it's not much of a secret. There wasn't a person at that party who couldn't see the way Nick was looking at you."

"He was looking at me?" she said lamely.

"Don't be coy. You know the look. Like he wants to devour you whole, without taking a breath. Like there wasn't another woman in the whole world but you." Julianna spread both hands on her stomach and leaned closer. "He's in love with you, Maggie."

Shocked, Maggie stared at Julianna. Love? That was ridiculous. He wanted her physically, he'd made that clear from the beginning. He'd even told her that he cared about her. But he didn't love her. Maggie was certain of that.

"Nick and I are...friends," she said carefully. It wasn't a complete lie. She'd like to think that they were friends, even if they were now lovers, as well.

Julianna smiled knowingly. "Okay, Maggie. I'm not trying to pry. But if you ever need an understanding ear, call me. Things were shaky for me and Lucas in the beginning, and nobody knows better than me how difficult these boys can be."

Maggie watched the "boys," as Julianna called them, all four of them, jump on a fumbled football and roll in the grass while the golden retriever barked and danced in circles around them. Nick held the ball up with a victorious shout, then Drew grabbed it from him, inciting a chase.

She smiled at their antics, then glanced back at Julianna, who was watching her carefully from under the brim of her hat. It felt good to sit here, under a blue sky, on the cool green grass and exchange "female" talk. She might not be able to tell Julianna the truth about her feelings for Nick, but it still felt good to talk to her about girl things.

Maggie poured two glasses of lemonade and handed one to Julianna. "You and Lucas are perfect for each other. I can't imagine you two ever being shaky."

A bright orange butterfly floated by on the warm breeze. Julianna sipped her lemonade and laughed softly. "Oh, we were shaky, all right. You want to know how Lucas proposed to me? He blackmailed me, that's how."

"Blackmailed you?"

Lips curved in a smile, Julianna nodded. "He thought he'd bullied me into marrying him, and I let him think that. The truth was I'd been desperately in love with him since I was fourteen. But that's another story for another time. Here come the children now."

Stunned by Julianna's confession, Maggie hadn't time to respond before the siege overtook them. Two small boys, two grown, muscled men and a yapping dog surrounded them.

"We're hungry," Drew announced. "Joshua's mom said he could eat with us if it's all right with you."

They dug into the food with the same enthusiasm they'd shown for football, even going so far as to toss chicken wings and the rolls that Julianna had brought. The frenzy made Maggie's head spin, and the wisecracks and insults exchanged between Nick and Lucas made her laugh.

She couldn't remember when she'd had such a good time. Or Drew. His cheeks bulged with food, and his eyes were bright with excitement. When the last cookie was gone, he ran off to play tanks and soldiers with Joshua and his dad. The golden retriever, Noah, ran at their heels.

Like sated warriors after a victory feast, Nick and Lucas stretched out their long legs, tucked their hands behind their heads and closed their eyes. Julianna and Maggie smiled at each other and shook their heads.

"So, Maggie—" Julianna brushed at the crumbs that seemed to forever find their way to her oversize stomach "—tell me about Roger."

"Roger?" Maggie glanced at Nick. He'd slitted one eye open. "Ah, what about him?"

"You know. Last night." She whispered, as if she didn't want the men to hear her, but there was a sparkle in her eyes. "You and Roger. In the bedroom."

Maggie felt the heat rush to her cheeks. Nick had both eyes open now, and he was scowling. Even Lucas was paying close attention, his gaze sleepy, but interested.

"There's not much to tell," Maggie hedged.

"That's not the way I saw it." Julianna reached for her lemonade. "You had that boy on his back so fast he never knew what hit him."

Maggie watched Nick rise up to his elbows and lock his dark, angry gaze on her. "What the hell is she talking about?"

"You mean you didn't tell him?" Julianna asked innocently, but the devil danced in her eyes.

"Tell me what?"

"There's really nothing to tell," Maggie began awkwardly. "I just—"

"She flipped him," Julianna finished, and delight brightened her face. "Knocked that boy right off his feet and threw him down flat on his back. There's been a Maggie Smith Fan Club started in her honor and I'm the president. We expect a lecture and detailed account of the momentous occasion at our first meeting."

Lucas chuckled and Nick glared at him. "You knew about this?"

"He'd still be lying in my guest bedroom if I hadn't helped him up," Lucas said cheerfully and winked at Maggie. "Sweet little Margaret Smith packs quite a wallop."

Nick stared at her, his lips pressed tightly together. He still had the nasty image of Roger with his hand on Maggie, his mouth close to hers when he'd been blocking her way at the gazebo. Nick had exercised tremendous restraint when he hadn't thrown the jerk over the railing and into the creek.

And now he found out that Roger had been bothering her again when she'd gone back into the house, and she'd handled it herself. Flipped the guy, for God's sake.

He knew it was unreasonable, but still, he couldn't stop the hot rush of anger heating his blood.

He stood, slapped his hat against his leg, then jammed it on his head. "I'm going to go check on the boys."

As he walked away, he heard Lucas chuckle again and decided he'd punch out his lights later.

He'd cooled down a little by the time he reached Drew and Joshua playing with the military action figures in the sand by the swings. Joshua's father and mother sat on a blanket nearby with a dark-haired toddler, a dimpled urchin in pink-flowered overalls and a matching baseball cap. They smiled and waved Nick over.

"Adam Wheeler." Joshua's father held out his hand.

"Nick Santos."

They shook hands, and Adam introduced his wife, Susan, a pretty brunette with apple cheeks and soft blue eyes. "Thanks for letting Joshua play with your son," Susan said. "We're new in Wolf River, and Josh doesn't know too many kids yet. We were hoping that you and your wife might allow Drew to come play one day after school."

They thought Drew was his son. And Maggie was his wife. Nick smiled at the thought, started to correct them, then decided to let it go. As strange as it seemed, he sort of liked the idea.

"I'll have to ask Maggie," he said, glancing over his shoulder at her. She was watching him, her expression concerned, but curious, as well. He reminded himself he was annoyed with her.

"We can't get over how much Drew looks like you," Susan said. "It's amazing."

Nick looked back at the woman and blinked. What had she said? That Drew looked like him? He held back a chuckle. He supposed he understood how people might see that. After all, they both had dark, almost black hair and eyes. And there was a similarity in the structure of their jaws. It was logical for people to assume that Drew was his.

Despite himself, he began to wonder again who Drew's father was, what he looked like. He wondered if maybe there was a resemblance between himself and the other guy. If maybe that was the reason that Maggie had such a strong, frightened reaction to him when she'd first seen him at the market. It would certainly make sense. Or worse, he thought with a scowl, if maybe she was attracted to him because he looked like the other guy. He didn't like that idea one little bit.

But he knew it was none of his business and that Maggie would resent any questions. He had no right to ask, no right at all to delve into her past. A past that she protected fiercely.

Still, he couldn't stop wondering.

Lucas and Julianna had gone for a walk by the time Nick joined Maggie back at the blanket.

"Still mad?" She sat with her arms wrapped around her bent legs and her chin on her knees. Her expression was innocent, pristine. Hardly the expression of a man-tossing, karate-flipping wild woman.

He decided to pout for a while. Maybe he'd get a kiss out of it. He stretched out beside her, angled his hat down to partially cover his face. "You could have at least told me about it."

"I could have."

"Well?"

"Well, what?"

He tipped his hat back up and frowned. "So tell me about it."

"There's nothing to tell. He cornered me in the bedroom when I went in to get my coat. I was in a bad mood, he put his hand on me, and I flipped him. End of story."

"So you didn't need my help out at the gazebo, then, did you? There I was, trying to save you from Roger, thinking that maybe he'd frightened you, and all along, you could have wiped the floor with the jerk. I'll bet you had a good laugh over that."

"No, Nick, I didn't have a good laugh over it at all." She turned her head, rested her cheek on her knee as she looked down at him. "I thought it was wonderful. I thought you were wonderful."

"Yeah?" Though it was small, he felt a slice of his pride return. "You thought I was wonderful?"

She nodded. "And sweet."

Sweet he wasn't sure about, but the tender, soft expression in those gorgeous green eyes as she gazed at him made his heart stop and his throat thicken with a feeling he couldn't quite identify. He stared back at her, felt his need for her rip through him like a knife.

"I'm going to kiss you, Maggie," he stated firmly. "Not now, because I won't be able to stop if I do. But later, when it's just you and me, I'm going to kiss you until you can't even remember your own name."

She sighed, then smiled softly. "Okay."

Ten

"I need you, Maggie. I'm lost without you. Please, I'll do anything. Just tell me what you want and I'll do it."

Maggie rolled her eyes and shifted the phone from one ear to the other while she tugged on her leather hiking boot. Thomas Crane, her boss at the paper, had been calling twice a day for the past three days.

"Thomas, I have ten more days on my leave. We've been over this. I can't leave until the doctor clears my father to drive again. That should be sometime next week."

"Maggie, I'm begging you," Thomas moaned into the phone. "David Brooks is out sick, Dan Howard is psychotic, and Georgia's threatening to quit."

"So what's the problem?" She heard the sound of phones ringing, then Georgia shrieking at Dan, then

Dan yelling back an obscenity that only made Georgia shriek louder. "Sounds like normal to me."

"Maggie, please, please, just listen to me..."

Only half listening to the same arguments he'd given her the past three days, she tugged on her other shoe while glancing at the sunflower clock over the stove in the kitchen. Nick was coming over at four, and it was already ten-to now. He hadn't said where they were going, just to wear jeans. Her insides were already churning with that same schoolgirl excitement she felt every time she saw him, which had been quite often since the day of the picnic. Too often, she knew, but had been powerless to say no to him.

Nick Santos was a man who knew how to get what he wanted. Which had turned out to be exactly what she'd wanted, as well, she thought with a slow smile.

But they hadn't just spent their time together in bed. They'd gone to the movies, to dinner, even bowling one night. Drew was included on early weekday outings, and last weekend there'd been a fishing trip, just the boys.

She'd known if she let Nick get this close, it was going to be difficult for both her and Drew to leave, but even she hadn't realized just how difficult. Drew would be devastated, she would be heartbroken. But somehow, as it had before, life would go on. At least now she'd have these wonderful memories.

"Maggie! Are you there? Are you listening to me? Answer me, dammit!"

Sighing, she went to tie her boot. "Yes, Thomas, I'm here, I'm listening. You need me. You want me to come home now. You'll give me anything I want."

Except he couldn't give her the one thing, the only thing she truly wanted. Nick.

She glanced up, saw him leaning against the kitchen doorway watching her. He wore jeans and a black leather jacket, white T-shirt and black boots. He absolutely took her breath away.

She stood too quickly, started to stumble backward, but he moved quickly and caught her, steadied her against his broad chest. His mouth lowered to hers, and he kissed her tenderly, a kiss filled with promise and anticipation.

"I've got to go, Thomas," she said breathlessly into the phone. "The house is on fire, and I've got to call the fire department."

"Don't hang up! Maggie, sweetheart, darling, I'm begging you, don't do—"

His lips still on hers, Nick took the phone from her and hung up. He ran his fingers through her hair and tugged her head backward so he could kiss her deeper still. She leaned into him, tasted the need humming between them. She was trembling when he pulled away.

"You want to tell me who called you 'sweetheart, darling' and wants you to come home and he'll give you anything you want?" he said evenly. "I need a name before I kill him."

"Thomas Crane, my boss. And you won't have to kill him. I'll do it myself." Her fingers were still shaking as she grabbed her jean jacket from the kitchen chair. "I didn't hear you knock."

"Your dad was standing at the curb with a sign that says Will Work for Cigar and Whisky. He told me to come on in."

She shook her head at his nonsense as she pulled her jacket on. "Just let me say goodbye to Drew and my mom."

He took hold of her arm when she started to move past him. "So are you?"

"Am I what?"

"Are you leaving?"

The intensity in his dark eyes and his voice made her heart pound. They hadn't discussed her leaving since that day in the park. There'd been no talk of the future, no whispered promises, no mention of anything beyond the relationship they shared now. Their time together had been fun and light, passionate, but there'd been an invisible line between them that neither one of them had crossed, a line that was as delicate as it was precarious.

They were standing on the edge of that line right now, and though she'd give anything to plunge head-first right over it, she couldn't. She'd shatter if she did. Not just her heart, but her entire being, her very soul. Because she was leaving, and nothing could stop that.

"Trying to get rid of me, Santos?" She forced her voice to be light, her smile to be easy.

His hand tightened on her arm. "Are you leaving?"

Her heart was like a drum now, heavy and hard against her ribs. His gaze ripped into her, and she saw something there, something that both frightened and thrilled her. "Not until my dad's driving," she said carefully, willing herself to keep the emotion out of her voice. "A few more days, at least."

"Nick!"

They both turned at the sound of Drew's excited greeting. He threw himself at Nick's legs and hugged. Her throat tight, she had to blink back the tears while she watched Nick kneel down, his fierce expression replaced with a wide grin for Drew.

She'd worried about Drew becoming too attached,

and that worry was now a reality. Two hearts would be broken when they left Wolf River and went back to New York, but it was too late to change that now.

"Hey, pal." Nick wrapped his arms around Drew. "How's it going?"

"Can you come to my school Friday and talk about your job? My teacher, Miss Perry, wants all the dads and moms to come and tell us kids what they do, and I know you aren't my dad but I asked my teacher if it was okay and she said sure you could come so can you?"

Nick had to rerun Drew's excited words through his brain again to figure it all out, then he rubbed the boy's head as he stood. "Sure, pal. If it's okay with your mom."

"It's okay with her, isn't it, Mom?" Drew looked hopefully at his mother.

Nick sensed the hesitation in Maggie and felt a swift stab of irritation. They had barely more than a week left before she went back to New York, and already she was drawing back inside herself, the same way she'd been before Lucas and Julianna's party. These past few days she'd been relaxed with him, comfortable. She'd forgotten that she wasn't interested in a relationship, that she didn't want to get involved. She'd laughed, opened up enough to share bits and pieces of her life, made love with him. But now he felt the wall going back up again, and it made him mad as hell.

Damn the woman, anyway. He was still bristling from overhearing her phone conversation with her boss, and here she was, as calm and cool as a blade of grass on a spring day. He felt a sudden overwhelming urge to kiss her senseless right here, right now. Then they'd see how cool and calm she was.

But he couldn't do that in front of Drew. He'd made a promise, and dammit to hell, he'd keep it.

"Well, can he, Mom? Can he?"

Maggie glanced at Nick, her smile wavering as she nodded. "Sure he can, sweetheart. If he has time."

"I have time," he said, but he felt that time was the one thing in the world he didn't have at all. It was running out quickly. Too damn quickly.

Maggie had shared passion with Nick, experienced intimately his uninhibited lust for life. He'd made her tremble, made her feel wanton and wild and free. But today was something else, something completely different.

Today he took her on her first motorcycle ride.

A real motorcycle ride, this time.

The wind whipped at her hair and face, raced over her skin. She clung to him, wrapped her arms tightly around his waist, pressed her body against his. Power hummed between her legs, heat and speed pumped furiously through her blood. Exhilarated, she screamed with delight as he roared down the highway, completely in control, master of the powerful machine beneath him.

"Where are we going?" she yelled in Nick's ear as they pulled off the highway and started to climb up into the mountains.

He didn't answer, just shifted gears as the road steepened and curved. As if they were one, she moved her body with his, pressed more tightly against him. Her breasts flattened against his wide, strong back, her thighs closed around his tight, firm butt. She felt as if she'd been turned inside out, with every raw nerve exposed. Adrenaline pumped through her veins, her pulse roared in her head, pounded behind her temples, her eyes and her ears. She'd never felt so completely and utterly alive.

They climbed higher into the mountains, where the dogwoods and pines grew thicker, until finally he slowed the bike down and pulled off the road onto a narrow dirt trail. Laughing, she held on tight as they bounced over the dips and bumps, following the trail several yards deeper into the forest. He stopped the bike behind an outcrop of boulders, tugged off his helmet, then turned to help her remove hers.

Shaking her hair, she took his hand as he helped her off the bike. Her knees were shaky, her legs weak, and she leaned against him when he slipped an arm around her shoulders.

"Where are we?" she asked, breathless as much from the ride as she was his closeness.

"Come on." He grabbed a rolled blanket from the back of the motorcycle, then took her hand and pulled her along behind him as he climbed up the wall of boulders.

When they reached the top, Maggie felt her breath catch.

As far as the eye could see stretched a green valley. A wide, winding creek separated the grassy land, and the setting sun sparkled silver in the swift moving water. Cattle dotted the landscape, their tails swishing and heads lowered while they munched lazily on the lush growth.

"Nick." She touched a hand to her throat. "It's so beautiful."

He spread the blanket out, then moved behind her, wrapping his arms around her while they stared out across the valley. "I thought you might like it."

"Who wouldn't?" She leaned back against the solid strength of his chest. If it were possible to make time stand still, this would be the moment. On top of a mountain, in Nick's arms, overlooking a lush valley. "How did you find this place?"

"By accident. I was thirteen and mad at the world. I'd been suspended from school for smoking behind the gym. I knew if I went home I was in for it, so I headed for the hills, so to speak. I rode my bicycle up here and found this spot. I came up here a lot after that."

"By yourself?"

"You mean, did I bring girls up here?" His lips brushed her ear, sent her pulse skittering through her veins.

"I was referring to Lucas and Ian," she said indignantly, though that was exactly what she'd meant. But she certainly didn't want him to know that.

"Sure you were." Chuckling, he nuzzled her neck. "But the answer is no on all counts. I never brought anyone here before. Lucas and Ian don't even know about it. I needed a place that was mine, just mine, where nothing and no one could get to me."

His place, she thought. *Just his.* And yet, he'd brought her here. Words failed her, and she turned to look at him, saw the flicker of memories in his eyes, of a childhood he'd rather forget. Of course he'd needed a place to be alone, a place where an alcoholic, abusive stepfather couldn't find him. Her heart ached for what he'd had to go through, but she felt anger, too. Anger at the stepfather, certainly, but even more at the mother who'd abandoned him.

There were tears in her eyes when she turned in his arms and slipped her arms around his waist. She held him, not as a lover, but as a friend. A simple, caring hug from one human being to another.

"Hey." He lifted her chin, touched the edge of her eyes with his fingertip and looked at the drop he'd pulled away. "What's this for?"

"I—"

I love you. She caught herself before the words came out. She couldn't tell him, she couldn't.

"I'm…so sorry," she said quietly. "Your mother…she left you with that horrible man. You were just a boy, you didn't deserve that."

He'd seen a woman's tears before, Nick realized. Angry tears, manipulative tears, tears of frustration. But never tears for *him,* tears for his lost childhood, for what had been robbed from him. His chest swelled; his throat tightened. Never had a woman so absolutely and completely humbled him.

He wiped at her tears with his thumbs. "We can't change the past, Maggie, and we can't know the future. We only have right now."

Even as the words were out, he realized that he'd been living his entire life in that belief. He'd denied the past, lived only in the present and never looked to tomorrow. And now, suddenly, with Maggie, tomorrow felt more important to him than any day ever had before. He wanted them to have tomorrow, and the day after that, and every day after that. He'd wanted them to have a future together, with Drew.

The thought staggered him. That he wanted Maggie, not just for now, but for always. Only Maggie, forever.

Good God, he was in love with her.

Really in love. Not just it-feels-good-for-the-moment love, but the big-*C* kind of love. The realization positively took the breath out of his lungs.

"Nick, what's wrong?"

He could only imagine the inane expression on his face as he stared at her. He knew this wasn't the time to tell her what he was thinking, what he was feeling. As skittish as she was, she would probably run back to New York and that idiot boss of hers.

She'd been abandoned once, left to care for her son by herself. He knew what that felt like, knew she was running from that kind of hurt again, just as he had his entire life. It was time for both of them to let go of the past, to learn how to trust. Together, they could do that. He wanted her, but more than that, he needed her. And Drew. He needed them both, in his life, in his heart.

He only had a few days left, but by God, he'd make her realize that she loved him, too. He'd be damned if he'd let her leave him.

She put her hands on his cheeks, and he blinked, brought himself back. There was concern in her knotted brow, sadness in her dusty green eyes. The tenderness in her touch made his throat feel thick and built a strange pressure in his chest.

"Maggie," he said raggedly as he dragged his fingers through her hair and tugged her head back. He touched his lips to the corners of her eyes, tasted the salt of her tears. "Have you any idea what you do to me?"

He lowered his mouth to hers, and she parted her lips on a sigh, welcomed him. Her arms slid around his neck as his hands moved down her back, over her buttocks, where he cupped her and lifted her, fitting her body to his. She was so soft, warm curves and smooth, silky skin. He eased them both to the blanket, let his body cushion hers as he brought her down with him. Her legs wrapped around him as he sat, and she strad-

dled him, pressed herself against him, moved her body
in rhythm with the same sensual dance of their tongues.

The breeze lifted her hair, and it fell around his face
like a satin curtain. He wanted to lose himself in her,
not just with his body, but with his very soul. He
tugged the hem of her tank top from her jeans, slid his
hands up her cool, flat stomach. She trembled at his
touch, moaned deep in her throat as he unclasped her
soft cotton bra and filled his hands with her breasts.

Gasping, she pulled her mouth from his and let her
head fall backward. Lips parted, eyes smoldering, she
locked her gaze with his while she tugged off her
denim jacket, then raised her arms over her head as she
pulled off her tank top. Blood pounded in his head as
he stared at her. Her hair tumbled around her shoulders,
shone like fire in the brilliance of the setting sun, her
skin glowed golden. Her breasts were high and firm,
rosy tipped, her nipples hardened with desire. She
looked like a goddess, and the sight of her offering
herself to him stole his breath away.

When he closed his mouth over one pearled, sensitive nipple she arched upward on a gasp. His tongue
teased, tasted, and she writhed under his touch. She
whispered his name over and over, her hands cupped
his face, then raked his scalp and buried themselves in
his hair, dragging him against her. He paid the same
loving attention to her other breast, tasted the sweetness
of her while the fire swept through his blood and loins.

Her hands, as restless as they were greedy, tugged
off his jacket, then tore his T-shirt from his jeans and
yanked it over his head. They were bare torso to bare
torso, and she moved over him, rubbed her breasts over

his chest, driving him mad with the sensation of her
hardened nipples over his heated skin. He took her
mouth again, reached for the snap of her jeans as she
reached for his.

He lay back, brought her with him, then ground his
teeth together on a low moan when her lips moved
down his chest, then lower. Her hands were fluid as
they skimmed over his hips; denim slid away. Her hair,
soft as silk, caressed his belly and thighs.

Surging upward, he sucked in a sharp breath and
buried his fingers in that glorious hair, called out her
name through tightly clenched teeth. His head swam,
his senses spun out of control, he swore he would break
apart under her touch. He had to be a part of her, be
inside her, he thought desperately, or he would certainly go mad.

On an oath, he pulled her up and with him as he
rolled, dragged her under him, his hands rough on her,
his mouth savage. When they were naked, he knelt over
her, moved between her legs while he watched her eyes
flare with desire. Threads of daylight still shimmered
around them, but an impatient moon was already on
the rise, trapping them between day and night, between
heaven and hell.

He slid into her, and then there was only heaven,
only Maggie. He lost himself there, felt her close
around him, draw him deep into ecstasy. There were
stars overhead. A cool breeze whispered over their
damp, heated skin, sang the music of the mountain, of
the trees, of the sky. This was home, this was life.
Everything that had ever been and would ever be. Maggie, only Maggie.

The sky was clear, but Maggie was certain that thun-
der had shaken the ground, that lightning had flashed

overhead. Surely they were caught in the eye of a storm, swept into the center of a tempest. Her senses reeled at the siege, swirled upward on a kaleidoscope of intense, fierce pleasure.

She heard him growl her name, felt the frenzy build with every soul-shattering thrust. Her nails raked his shoulders, and she took him still deeper into her body, into her heart. Her breath came in quick, shallow gasps, her heart slammed furiously in her chest. The feelings were as wild, as untamed as the mountains surrounding them, and she gave herself up to them, let herself go as she never had before. Love sang in her blood and pounded in her temples. There was only Nick. No one else before, no one after. Only Nick.

Lifting her hips to him, she cried out, felt her body go taut, felt the shudders rip through her even as he answered her. Unrestrained, the passion rolled through them like a powerful wave. The mountain and valley echoed with the rapture and the joy, then went blissfully quiet.

They lay twined in each others' arms, the air slowly cooling their damp, heated bodies. Maggie shivered when a breeze danced over her skin, then fussed when Nick moved away from her. He covered her with the edge of the blanket, then gathered her in his arms again. She snuggled against him, felt the deep, heavy thud of his heart against hers and smiled at the peace and contentment curling through her.

"Wow," he whispered harshly.

She laughed softly. Hardly poetic, but certainly an accurate description. "Yeah," she murmured. "Wow."

There were other words that came to mind, as well. *Love. Happy. Bliss.*

Deception.

The word balled like a fist in her stomach. How could she allow herself to feel happy, to feel bliss, when there were lies between them, unforgivable lies? Didn't Nick deserve more than that?

The breeze whipped over them again, and the trees shook their branches at her like accusing fingers. The peace she'd felt only a moment ago turned to cold dread. He did deserve more, she knew, but she wasn't sure she had the courage to give it to him.

Eleven

He had the dream again. This time, more real than ever before. He was in the forest. It was dark, with moonlight filtering through the trees. He held the woman in his arms, tasted the wine on her lips, felt her smooth, silky skin under his fingertips. Heard her deep, throaty sigh. Like before, he couldn't see her face, couldn't speak to her.

A mist crept over the forest floor, thickened, then slithered upward like dark, gray fingers. The woman turned from him, stepped into the fog. He called to her, but no sound came out. He tried to follow, but his legs wouldn't move. And like every time before, he woke, his body drenched with sweat, his heart pounding.

On a curse, Nick sat, flipped on the bedside table light and raked his hands through his hair. Four in the morning. Damn. Always 4:00 a.m. He drew in a slow, deep breath and let it out again, waited for his hands to stop shaking before reaching for his jeans. He wouldn't sleep, he knew that by now. He might as well do something useful, something productive, like pace.

Stumbling to the kitchen, he set the coffeepot brewing. He made it strong, triple strength. Caffeine always did the trick, always kick started his blood and pulled the sleep out of his brain.

But it was so real this time, he thought, rubbing a hand over his bare chest. He could still smell her perfume, hear her softly call his name. He just couldn't see her face.

He knew the woman wasn't Maggie. He'd had the dream for almost five years now, ever since that night with his mystery lady. But he'd never had it so often, with such intensity, as he'd had since Maggie had shown up.

He was certain that the dream's frequency was due to the fact she was leaving next week. Leaving him, just as his mystery lady had. He was frustrated beyond belief, on edge and irritated that Maggie had shown no sign of changing her mind, no sign of hesitation or even reluctance. Last night, when he'd taken her and Drew for ice cream in town, she'd casually mentioned New York several times, even talked about her job: subjects that she never discussed without being prompted. He knew what she was doing, that she was gently telling him that their time together was coming to an end.

He narrowed his eyes at the thought. She had another think coming.

Opening the kitchen drawer, he pulled out a small black velvet box. His hand shook as he opened the lid with his thumb, stared at the diamond ring inside. The solitaire sparkled in the soft glow of the overhead fluorescent light. His insides knotted.

He was going to ask her to marry him tomorrow night. He'd already planned a romantic, candlelight dinner at Adagio's in the Four Winds Hotel. He'd even gone so far as to reserve a suite, to celebrate after she said yes, though he realized that he was taking a gamble on that one. But hell, life was full of gambles. He'd always been a risk taker, hadn't he?

With his life maybe, with his body, but never with his heart.

He'd never been so terrified in his entire life.

What if she said no? If she took Drew and they really left? He'd come to care for the boy, more than he'd thought possible. They were a package, the two of them. A beautiful, brightly colored package complete with ribbons and bows. He wanted them, both of them, more than he'd ever wanted anything in his life.

He should be furious at her. He'd been more than content before she came along, perfectly satisfied with his life, who he was, what he was. He'd taken each day in stride, enjoying the moment before moving on to the next. Nothing ever rattled him for more than a few hours, nothing ever got under his thick skin.

Until Maggie. She'd gotten under his skin, then deeper, into his heart, his soul. Into that place inside himself where no one had ever gone before, where he'd never let anyone in. A place that a frightened, lonely, ten-year-old boy had closed off long ago.

The diamond in his hand winked at him. He stared at it for a long moment, then closed his hand around the velvet box. The lid snapped shut like a trap, echoed in the quiet of the room. Today was career day at Wolf River Elementary. His chest tightened as he remembered Drew asking him to come and talk, even though he wasn't his dad.

What would Drew say, Nick wondered, if he told him that he wanted to make a career out of being his dad? That he wanted to marry his mom and spend the rest of their lives together?

Releasing a long, deep breath, he slipped the box back into the drawer and reached for a mug, poured himself a cup of thick, black coffee and began to prepare himself for what was about to be the most important day of his life.

"How do I look?"

"Fishing for a compliment, Santos?" Maggie smoothed the collar of Nick's navy button-up shirt, not because it needed it, but because she couldn't resist touching him.

They stood backstage in the Wolf River Elementary auditorium. Maggie had already spoken about her job as a journalist and writer, then they'd listened to a librarian, a rancher and an ear, nose and throat doctor. The current speaker, an accountant, had the children squirming in their seats and whispering amongst themselves. Nick was the final speaker, and Maggie was certain that Miss Perry had saved the best for last.

"How 'bout a kiss for luck, then?" Nick lowered his face to Maggie's. Frowning, she pushed him back with the palm of her hand on his chest.

"There are children present. Behave yourself."

He straightened with a sigh, then lowered his voice and leaned close again. "Okay, so how 'bout we go over to my place after we're done here?"

A shiver slithered up her spine at his suggestive tone. She shook her head. "I'm taking my father to the doctor at eleven, then having lunch with Julianna."

"It's only ten o'clock," he whispered seductively. "We have time to…"

Maggie held her breath as he whispered, in detail, what he had in mind. Heat flooded through her veins, warmed her skin under the cool beige silk pantsuit she wore. In spite of herself, in spite of where they were, she felt her body respond.

"Nick Santos!"

At Miss Perry's call, Maggie jumped, then stepped quickly back, feeling as if she'd been caught playing hanky-panky on school grounds. But Miss Perry, an attractive brunette with big blue eyes, had her gaze locked on to Nick and had barely acknowledged Maggie's presence.

"You're next, Nick." Miss Perry beamed at him. "The children are all so excited that you're here."

The children weren't the only ones excited, Maggie thought irritably as the pretty teacher batted her eyes. Good heavens, did the woman have to be so obvious? But then, Maggie realized with more than a twinge of understanding, what woman didn't react that way to Nick?

Maggie didn't want to think about all the women like Miss Perry, whom Nick would turn his attention to after she was gone. It was difficult enough that she would be leaving next week, why torment herself with thoughts of Nick with other women? She'd promised herself that she would live in the moment, enjoy the time they had together, and even if it killed her, dammit, that was exactly what she intended to do.

"Oh, Maggie," Miss Perry said, as if she suddenly realized that she and Nick weren't alone. "We're taping the speakers today as a little memento for each child. Would you mind checking the volume, then turning it on Record after I introduce Nick?''

"Sure.'' Maggie smiled, took the cassette recorder the teacher handed her and resisted the urge to scowl at the woman when she took Nick's arm and led him away. The accountant was still speaking, something about the thrill of learning to balance checkbooks, when Miss Perry came out and asked if there were any questions. There weren't. While the teacher thanked the man, Maggie tested the volume on the cassette player, set it to record and placed it on a chair at the edge of the stage.

When she looked up again, Nick caught her eye and winked. He was incorrigible, she thought, shaking her head. Uncontrollable and unpredictable. And for the next few days, she thought with a mixture of pleasure and grief, he was all hers.

"All right, children.'' Miss Perry raised her hands to quiet the room. "Everyone please pay attention now. Drew Hamilton has asked a special friend to come visit with us today, and we need to be on our best behavior while he's speaking. Can we all say good morning to Mr. Santos?''

"Good morning, Mr. Santos,'' over two hundred small voices echoed in the auditorium as Nick stepped up to the microphone. When he cupped a hand to his ear and told the kids he couldn't hear them, they all screamed louder, making the sound system reverberate. When he grabbed his chest and stumbled backward, the children howled with laughter.

Ham, Maggie thought as she rolled her eyes. Not that she was surprised. After all, he'd raced and performed exhibitions in front of thousands, been on the cover of at least half a dozen high-profile magazines and posed for at least two well-known clothes manufacturers. Nick Santos was not a shy man.

What he was, was sexy, charming, fun and dropdead handsome. A dangerous combination for any man, but for Nick, it was downright deadly.

She watched him clown it up for the kids, describe how he'd turned something he'd enjoyed doing into a job. He stressed that money shouldn't be the reason you choose a job, but that first and most important, you should like what you do. That if you liked your job, it would be fun and never feel like work.

Her own job felt like work, she realized. Thomas had been calling twice daily, and even though she enjoyed what she did, the thought of going back to the chaos of her office made her head ache.

Almost as much as her heart ached.

She moved to the edge of the stage, just inside the curtains, and scanned the room until she found Drew. He had a wide smile on his face, his big eyes were glued onto the man speaking at the microphone. Her son adored Nick, talked about him endlessly. She knew how hard it was going to be on him when they left.

She felt the moisture in her eyes, blinked it away. It was bad enough she'd let herself fall in love with Nick all over again, but she'd dragged Drew in, as well. That was unforgivable.

Almost as unforgivable that she'd kept father and son apart all these years.

Since that day on the mountaintop, she'd known she had to tell Nick the truth. She realized that he might never speak to her again, that he might refuse to claim Drew as his own, but she couldn't lie to him anymore. Drew and Nick both deserved a chance. They both deserved to make their own choices. She had to accept whatever the consequences might be.

Coward that she was, she'd planned on waiting until the day before she and Drew were leaving. There would be anger, she was certain of it, and she didn't want Drew exposed to the turmoil or confusion.

But as she watched Nick banter with the kids, watched him point to Drew and say hello, then Drew's excited wave back, she knew she couldn't wait. If Nick believed her, if he accepted Drew as his own, then the next few days would be important to both Nick and Drew as father-son time. She couldn't take that away from him, no matter how frightened she was of the outcome. There was no question in her mind that it was too late for Nick and her, but there might still be a chance for Drew and Nick.

He was talking about the importance of school and an education when she turned away on shaky knees. She couldn't face him now, she needed a little time by herself before she took her father to the doctor. Time to think, to find the right words.

She prayed her words would be the right ones.

Nick gave the motorcycle full throttle on the last stretch before he turned into the parking lot of his shop. For good measure, he popped a wheelie, then spun three figure eights before sliding sideways ten feet through a wide shallow puddle. Water sprayed, a flock of sparrows scattered. The motorcycle stopped six inches from the entrance.

Damn, but he was in a good mood.

And why shouldn't he be? He'd had his first school function as a dad—well, *almost* a dad—and he was about to ask the woman he loved to marry him. It was the same feeling he'd always had before every race. That same nerves-on-edge, adrenaline-pumping, fire-in-his-gut feeling.

He always went into every race absolutely knowing that he would win. Asking Maggie to marry him would be no different, he decided. She'd say yes. She *had* to say yes. He couldn't think any other way.

He knew he wouldn't be able to concentrate on his work now, even though he was three weeks behind and had customers screaming at him. They could go somewhere else if they didn't like it.

He looked at his watch. Damn. It was only ten forty-five. Their dinner reservations weren't until eight, and he wouldn't pick Maggie up until seven forty-five. What the hell was he supposed to do for nine hours? He felt the power of the motorcycle under him, thought about riding into the mountains. That would burn off some of this energy, calm him down and give a little balance to his spinning world.

He sighed heavily and tugged off his helmet. No, he couldn't go into the mountains. Now that he'd taken Maggie there, he'd only think of her. She'd be with him, whispering over his shoulder, and he'd want her so badly he'd go crazy.

Anxious, he paced the shop, stopping to check the installation of an engine he'd worked on yesterday. Then, restless again, he moved into his office where his answering machine blinked furiously at him. Ten calls. Damn. Damn.

All right. He'd do some paperwork, make a few calls. That would kill a little time. He was reaching for the phone when he realized that the cassette Drew's teacher had given him was still in his shirt pocket. He reached behind him and popped it into his stereo, then turned back around and started to dial the phone.

His hand froze.

"Cottleston, Cottleston, Cottleston pie, a fly can't bird, but a bird can fly…testing, testing, testing…"

He turned slowly, stared at the stereo in confusion. How had he gotten the wrong tape? Two seconds later he heard Miss Perry's voice, then his own as he greeted the children. This was the right tape, all right.

He rewound the tape, turned it louder as he played it again. The voice was soft, smooth, clear. Sexy.

Maggie?

Miss Perry had handed the cassette player to Maggie and asked her to record his talk. He narrowed his eyes, remembering that he had watched her test the volume just before he went on stage.

He played it again, closed his eyes and played it again.

Something passed through him. Something intangible, with no substance, yet it held him tighter than steel chains. He rose, went into his bedroom and dug through a box he kept under his bed, an odd assortment of photos, racing medals and memorabilia. He found the cassette he was looking for and came back into the office.

He played the old cassette.

"Cottleston, Cottleston, Cottleston pie…"

Frowning, he stared at the two cassettes. They were identical, except the voice in the old cassette was quieter, shook just a little.

What in the world was going on?

Maybe the silly saying was common, a phrase everyone used to test a recorder, just like everyone always

typed out, "Now is the time for all good men to come
to the aid of their country."

But it was the same voice. The mystery woman's
and Maggie's. They sounded exactly alike.

As if they were the same woman.

He sat, staring, for what felt like a lifetime, before
he picked up the phone again.

Nick's shop was quiet when Maggie stepped inside
an hour later. No generator motor running, no air tools.
No loud rock music blaring from the radio. He hadn't
even turned the overhead lights on in the shop, or in
his office. If his motorcycle and truck both weren't outside, she might have thought he wasn't even here.

"Nick?"

She moved through the shop, into the office, jumped
when she saw him sitting in his office chair, in the near
dark. He said nothing, didn't move, just stared at her
with unblinking eyes.

It had been less than two hours since she'd seen him,
but she knew that something was terribly wrong. "Are
you all right?"

"Sit down, Maggie."

His voice, so cold, so distant, like his eyes, terrified
her. She sank slowly onto the chair across from his.
"What's wrong?" she asked, certain she didn't want
to hear the answer.

"When were you going to tell me?"

Her fingers were cold as she folded them in her lap.
"Tell you?"

"About Drew."

Fear snaked through her blood. "Drew?"

His eyes glinted like onyx, his jaw tightened. "That
he's my son."

Oh, dear God. She gripped the arms of her chair, felt her throat close up on her.

How could he know? It wasn't possible.

He turned, flipped on the cassette player behind him. She heard her own voice, repeating that silly Winnie the Pooh rhyme. Confused, she simply looked at him. "I-I made that this morning."

He shook his head slowly. "You made that five years ago. When you were working for the *North Carolina Tribune.* You were assigned to interview me after my race, and you left it in the room. I kept it as a little memento of a great night of sex with a nameless, faceless woman. Tell me, Maggie, is that how you interviewed all the men you were assigned? You crawled into bed with them, then left without even telling them your name?"

She felt the blood drain from her face and turn to a knot of ice in her stomach. "No," she whispered, shook her head and repeated, "No."

He still hadn't moved, but he had the look of a stalking panther. The tension in the room was a living, breathing thing.

"After I heard this tape," he said evenly, his voice edge with steel, "it was easy to track you. The papers you worked for and past references brought me right back to North Carolina at exactly the same time I was there." He picked up a sheet of paper from the top of his desk. "Your old boss was even so helpful as to fax me a copy of the article the paper ran. An article that gave explicit details of the race, even the party afterward. Written by M. J. Smith."

She winced when he tossed the paper at her. Anger narrowed his eyes, pressed a hard line across his mouth. "Why, Maggie, just tell me why. Were you playing some kind of sick game? The same game you've been playing since you came back to Wolf River?''

"No," she choked out. "You have to believe me."

"Believe you?" he snorted. "Lady, the last thing I'd ever do is believe you."

A sob filled her chest, but she forced it back down. She was standing at the doorway to hell, and there was nothing she could do but walk in.

"Five years ago," she said, her voice shaking, "I was terrified when my boss assigned you to me. I never even told him that we knew each other. With all your success and the kind of life you led, I didn't even think you'd remember a simple, plain girl like Maggie Smith, anyway."

Nick made a rude sound, but he didn't interrupt, just kept those dark, furious eyes locked on her.

"When I walked into the celebration party in your suite, I was overwhelmed. I was going to leave again, but a blond man in a Hawaiian shirt thought I was from the hotel, that I'd come to inspect a problem you'd reported in the bathroom. I tried to explain, but it was loud and I was nervous, so I ended up in your bathroom, drinking champagne. It relaxed me, gave me a shot of courage to go ahead with the interview. I made that silly tape and was on my way out when you came in and shut off the light. When you said you saw me and you were glad I was there..."

She stopped, felt her cheeks flame with humiliation, then cleared her throat and continued. "I was stupid enough to think you actually knew who I was. Then when you kissed me, I couldn't think at all. I simply believed what I wanted to believe. That a man like you could have wanted a woman like me."

"You just left," he said tightly.

"You called me another woman's name," she whispered hoarsely. "I was humiliated. I'd made a fool out of myself. How could I have ever faced you again?"

"You were pregnant, dammit!" He stood, slammed his hands on the desk. The phone rattled, and a stack of papers flew.

"It was six weeks before I found out." Her voice felt raw, every ragged breath burned. "You'd been long gone, back on the racing circuit. By the time I worked up the courage to call you, you were knee-deep in a paternity suit. You would have thought me just one more lovesick groupie crawling out of the woodwork. I couldn't stand the thought of fingers pointing, of my picture plastered all over the tabloids. I would have lost my job, and then how would I take care of my baby?"

"*Our* baby," he snapped. "I had a right to know."

"Nick, you didn't even know you'd made love to me. If I'd come to you, would you have believed that the woman in your bed was boring little Maggie Smith?"

He pushed away from the desk, moved to the windows overlooking the shop and stared out. She rose from her chair, steadied herself with a hand on his desk and turned toward him. His back was to her, his shoulders stiff. Her fingers ached to touch him.

"You were a virgin," he said without emotion.

"Yes."

His hands knotted into fists. "And did you think that meant nothing to me?" he asked harshly. "Did you think I led such a life of debauchery that luring innocent women to my bed was just another day in the life?

You were pregnant, dammit, with my child. You had no right to keep that from me."

"I didn't know you." He still wouldn't look at her, and it was ripping her insides. "I could only imagine the life you led, the women. Even if I convinced you that Drew was yours, if there was positive proof, I couldn't imagine that you would welcome a child into that life. I didn't want to force a child on you, a child you'd never asked for."

"So you kept him," he said bitterly.

She glanced up sharply. "There was never any question that I would keep him. I loved him from the moment I knew he was growing in me. I made a decision to raise him myself."

"You forgot about Richard." His words dripped with sarcasm.

"I already told you that Richard was a mistake, that I thought Drew needed a father. Even for Drew, it was wrong to marry someone I didn't love."

"You're just full of mistakes, aren't you, Maggie?"

"I'm sorry, Nick." She pushed away from the desk, took a shaky step toward him. "If you want him to, maybe Drew could visit you occasionally. He wouldn't even have to stay with you. He could stay at my parents', and you could come see him when you could manage the time."

She gasped as he swung around and took hold of her arms. "Visit him occasionally?" He spat the words at her. "Manage the time?"

He released her, and she stumbled back. She felt numb, exhausted, but she steadied herself, then straightened and faced him. "You have every right to be furious with me. But please, I'm begging you, don't hate Drew, too. He loves you."

I love you, she desperately wanted to say. But he would never believe her now. As he'd already told her, he would never believe anything she told him.

"Hate Drew?" Astonishment furrowed his brow as he dragged a hand through his hair. "You think I could hate him? Is that how little you think of me?"

His anger was one thing that she could somehow handle and come to terms with, but the disgust in his eyes, the revulsion was her undoing. Frantic, she reached out to him. "Nick, listen to me, please—"

He stepped away from her, held up one hand as a warning to stay back. "No, Maggie. You listen. An hour ago I was ready to beg you to stay here in Wolf River. You and Drew. I thought I'd fallen in love with you. I even wanted to marry you. Imagine that—" his laugh was dry and hoarse "—you made a chump out of me not once, but twice. That's pretty damn impressive for plain little old Maggie Smith."

She didn't bother to wipe at the tears falling down her cheeks. "Nick—"

"You had your turn, Maggie," he said tightly. "Now it's my turn. The only one who's going to be *visiting* Drew from now on will be you."

She felt the blood drain from her face again, turn to ice as it settled in her stomach. "What are you saying?"

"That you can go back to New York, I don't much give a damn. But you're not taking Drew. You robbed me of more than four years of my son's life, and I don't plan on missing out on one more day. And I don't doubt for one second that any judge will disagree with me on this one."

She felt the room spin around her, the ground shift under her. This wasn't happening. It couldn't be. "You can't do that," she whispered between painful breaths. "You can't take him away from me."

"Don't worry, Maggie, you'll have your *visits*." He stepped closer, ran his finger over her jaw, then roughly cupped her chin in his hand. "Who knows, darlin', maybe you can crawl into my bed again one of these days, too."

She jerked her head away at his ugly words. Maybe she deserved all of this, his hatred, his scorn, but losing her son was inconceivable. She would never let that happen. Never.

She straightened, lifted her chin. "Don't do this, Nick," she said quietly, leveling her gaze with his. "Please don't do this."

He turned away from her. "You wouldn't want to be late for your lunch date, Maggie. Just close the door on your way out."

The urge to beg, to drop to her knees and plead with him to listen to her, to believe her, overwhelmed her. But the stiff, cold set of his shoulders stopped her. What good would it do? She might as well try to cut down an oak with a butter knife. He wouldn't listen to her, wouldn't believe her. He never would.

She turned, surprised that her legs were still able to carry her, and walked woodenly away. Outside, as she reached for her car door, she swore she heard the shattering of glass, and was certain it was her heart.

Twelve

He wanted to get drunk. Rip-roaring, fried-to-the-tonsils, drop-dead drunk. And he intended to. Just not yet. Right now he wanted to feel the pain, wanted to feel the sharp, deep bite of every lie. It fed his anger, fueled the rage inside him. That anger was the only thing he had to hold on to, the only thing that felt alive in him at the moment. The only thing that kept him going.

That and the knowledge he had a son.

Drew, with the big, dark eyes and shiny hair. *My* eyes. Nick swiped a hand across his desk, sent the phone flying across the office. *My* hair. A coffee mug with pencils was Nick's next victim. It exploded against the wall.

Drew was his son. His and Maggie's.

He'd gone numb when the truth had finally sunk in. Even while he'd been making the phone calls to the newspapers where Maggie had worked, he'd told himself there had to be an explanation of some kind. That the whole situation was just some weird coincidence. He even expected they'd have a laugh about it later.

Some laugh.

Fists clenched, he turned at the sharp crunch of glass behind him. Lucas stood outside the office, hands on his hips while he inspected emptiness where the glass wall had been.

Lucas tipped his Stetson back and squinted at one jagged edge of glass protruding from its frame. "Remodeling?"

"My foot slipped," Nick growled.

Lucas glanced around the office, at the strewn papers, broken mug and smashed phone, then looked calmly back at Nick.

Nick wanted Lucas to say something, anything, so that he could turn his anger on him. He suspected that was why he'd called Lucas to come over, to release some pent-up frustration with his fists. But they'd known each other too long. Lucas knew when to talk and when to wait. Right now he waited.

"Drew is my son."

There. He'd just blurted it out. He realized it felt good to say it out loud.

Lucas raised his eyebrows and whistled softly. "I take it you didn't know?"

"How the hell could I have known?" he snapped. "Less than two hours ago, I didn't even know that Maggie and I had slept together."

Lucas narrowed his eyes and tilted his head in disbelief. "You wanna talk about that one?"

Nick dragged both hands through his hair and sighed heavily. "Yeah," he said quietly. "I guess I do."

He paced while he told Lucas everything he'd managed to piece together from his phone calls and Maggie's confession. How she'd ended up in his bed, how he hadn't known it was her. Her reasoning why she'd never told him. Here and there he'd punctuate his story by kicking the wall or smashing his fist on his desk. All the while, Lucas kept his head bent, listening.

"I've lost more than four years of my own son's life, dammit," Nick said when he'd finished. "His first word, his first step, birthdays, Christmas. How the hell will I ever make up for that?"

Lucas shook his head. "That thinkin' won't take you any farther than a rocking horse, Nick. Seems to me you need to think about right now."

"That's exactly what I'm doing," Nick shot back. "I don't intend to miss one more day of Drew's life. He's coming to live with me."

"What about Maggie?" Lucas asked quietly.

"What about her?" Nick felt a fresh stab of pain rip through him. "You think I give a damn now, after what she did?"

"Yeah, I do think you give a damn." Lucas stared at the broken glass and disheveled office. "I think you give one big hell of a damn."

"Don't tell me what I think," Nick shouted. "You're supposed to be my friend, dammit. If I say I don't give a damn, you damn well better agree with me or you'll be picking your damn teeth out of your ears."

Lucas grinned slowly, braced himself for what was about to come. "You're right, Nick. The woman's no good. She lies and she obviously sleeps around. You don't want to get mixed up with a woman like that. Whatever attraction you had, it was obviously just in bed. With that face and body, what red-blooded man wouldn't want a toss in the sheets with her? Damn, if I wasn't married I sure—''

Because he'd been ready for it, Lucas was able to dodge the fist that came at his face. But his foot slid on a chunk of glass when Nick rammed him, and they both went sliding across the concrete. Lucas's hat took flight with Nick's next punch, which riled Lucas to no end. Still, he let Nick have one more punch, then decided to put the boy out of his misery.

The hit to Nick's chin was solid and direct. His head snapped back, and he had to blink away the stars that exploded in front of his eyes. Certain that the room was moving around him, he decided to retain at least a modicum of dignity and sit rather than fall. He landed backward on his butt in a pile of tires. So much for dignity.

So much for pride.

''Now here's what I really think.'' Lucas retrieved his hat, then brushed off his jeans and sat on a stack of tires beside Nick. ''I think you're blind in love with Maggie. I think you should end all this misery you're in and just marry the woman. Any fool, and that most certainly includes you, Nickie boy, could see she's blind in love with you, too. Everything else will work itself out. Trust me on this one, pal. I've been there.''

Nick didn't believe it for a minute. His heart was in more pieces than the engine on his workbench, but at least an engine he knew how to put back together again and make it run. Better than before, even. He'd taken the edge off his anger with Lucas, but these other feelings were completely foreign to him. He hadn't a clue what to do with them.

White-knuckled, he raked his fingers through his

scalp. "She's going back to New York next week. Taking Drew with her. How the hell we supposed to work that out?"

"You talk to her, for a start." Lucas jammed his hat on his head. "Where is she now?"

He remembered the look in her eyes when he'd told her that he was going to take Drew away from her. Her face had gone pale, her lips had trembled. At the moment, he'd enjoyed the pain, the terror he'd caused her. Now he felt sick.

He dropped his head into his hands. "She had a lunch date with Julianna, but she might have canceled. She was pretty upset when she left."

"I can't imagine why," Lucas said with enough sarcasm to make Nick want to hit him again. "Especially after you told her you were going to take Drew away. How do you know she didn't run?"

He shook his head. "She won't leave until her dad gets the okay to drive."

His head went up as he remembered that she'd taken her father to the doctor this morning. He'd been too absorbed with discovering that Drew was his son, that she'd lied to him, to think about what she might do.

"Julianna was getting dressed when I left an hour ago. I'll call and see if she's still there. Good thing I carry my own phone," Lucas said with a grin. "Seeing's how yours is in little pieces, kind of like your heart."

Nick scowled at Lucas, but was just too damn tired to hit him now. There would always be later.

"Damn." Lucas patted his shirt pocket where he carried his small cell phone.

"What?"

"My phone slipped out when you tackled me."

They found it five minutes later behind an oil drum, but it took another ten to get the grease out of the buttons and make it work.

"No answer." Lucas listened to his answering machine, left a message, then dialed the restaurant. They weren't there, either. Lucas frowned at the phone after he hung up. "Strange that Julianna didn't call and cancel. I think I'll go home and check it out. In the meantime, why don't you go find Maggie? Just talk to her, Nick. You've got nothing to lose."

Nick sat there for a long time after Lucas left, staring blankly at the wall. Lucas was right about one thing, Nick thought miserably. He had nothing to lose, because he'd already lost it all.

"Sweetheart, this isn't the answer," Angela Smith folded the last sweater in the pile Maggie had made and handed it to her.

"It's the only answer, Mom." Maggie closed the last suitcase, tucked her purse over her shoulder, then took her mother's hands. "I'm sorry I never told you any of this before. I didn't want to shame you any more than I already had. Please forgive me."

"There's nothing to forgive, Maggie." Tears were in Angela's eyes as she pulled her daughter into her arms. "We're so very proud of you. We always have been. We love you and Drew so much."

Maggie wiped at her own tears. She'd been crying all the time she'd packed her and Drew's bags, all the time she'd told her mother the truth, the whole truth. She would have thought there were no tears left by now. Obviously she'd been wrong. But then, this was apparently her day to be wrong.

She was running. That might be wrong, too. But she

didn't know what else to do but get as far away from Nick as possible. She was certain he was furious enough to follow through on his threat to take Drew, and she could never let that happen. If she had to quit her job and move ten times, then she would. No one, not even Nick, would ever take her son away from her.

She'd rescheduled her flight, and it was leaving in one hour. It would be close, but she'd make it. She had to. She had to leave now, before there were any more ugly confrontations with Nick. The hatred, the anger, the disgust she'd seen in his eyes. She couldn't survive that again.

The only reason she would survive at all was Drew. He was her lifeline, her reason for living, her whole being. Nick had been, too, but that was gone now. She hoped that one day she'd be able to remember the good times they'd shared, the picnic, the mountaintop, making love.

One day, maybe. But not now. Now she could only think of leaving. Of being strong for Drew.

He'd cried all afternoon, too. He didn't want to leave. He'd wanted to stay with Grandma and Grandpa. With Nick. She had no idea how a heart already broken could break again, but hers had. She'd been thankful at least that he'd cried himself to sleep. Something she intended to do as soon as they were home.

When the suitcases were finally in the car, and a sleeping Drew buckled into the back seat, Maggie kissed her father goodbye. As usual, he said little, but she felt a fierceness when he pulled her into his arms, a strength she'd never noticed before.

There were more tears and hugs with her mother until Maggie finally drove away. She had almost passed the road leading to Blackhawk Circle Ranch when she remembered her lunch date with Julianna. She had to say goodbye to her. Julianna had been a good friend, and no matter what happened, Maggie wanted her to know that she cared about her, that she appreciated her friendship.

She turned off the road, promised herself five minutes as she parked in front of the house and shut off the engine. The house was quiet, no answer to her knock or the doorbell. She'd turned to leave when a soft, muffled sound from inside caught her ear.

"Julianna?" She knocked again, then carefully opened the front door and called again.

There it was again, only louder this time. A soft cry. From the guest bedroom. Maggie hurried down the short hall, pushed open the door to the room.

"Julianna!"

"Maggie! I know you're in there. Open the door!"

He'd been knocking for five minutes, pounding for two. She had to be here, he thought furiously. She wasn't with Julianna, and considering the frame of mind she'd been in when she'd left him, she wouldn't have gone anywhere else.

He held his finger down on the doorbell. Where *was* she, dammit!

And where were her parents? They were always home. They had to know the whole story by now, as well. They wouldn't have let Maggie drive anywhere in the condition she was in.

Cupping his hands around his face, he moved to the front window and peered in. He only had a view of the dining room and kitchen, but they were empty.

Swearing under his breath, he stormed to the garage to look for cars, but it was locked. The backyard, he decided. Mrs. Smith was always out back working with her flowers. He was halfway to the side gate when he caught a movement at the edge of the fence between the Smiths and their neighbor.

He stepped up on a wooden crate beside the wood fence and looked over. It was Mrs. Potts, the elderly next door neighbor, holding a fat tabby in her arms while she tried to peek around the edge of the fence.

"Mrs. Potts?"

The fragile, slender woman jumped at Nick's call, then whirled, eyes wide behind her silver-framed glasses. "Y-yes?"

"Mrs. Potts, have you seen Maggie?"

The tabby meowed irritably when Mrs. Potts hugged her tighter. "I mind my own business, Nick Santos," the woman said defensively. "I'm a good neighbor, keep to myself."

He thought it best not to remind her she'd been snooping around the fence. "I'm sure you do, Mrs. Potts. I just want to know if you've seen Maggie today."

"Well..." She hesitated, then bit her bottom lip. "Actually, I did see her."

Nick thought he might scream. Clenching his jaw, he forced a smile. "Recently?" he prodded.

"Maybe an hour ago. Packed up her bags and that boy of hers and left here lickety-split. All those tears and hugs. Made my heart ache just watching them say goodbye." She petted the tabby's head. "Little Drew used to pet my Scarlett here."

Packed her bags? Took Drew? Nick gripped the top slat of the fence so hard he heard wood crack. He fought back his panic, knowing if he frightened the elderly woman, she'd run for her back door and he'd never get any information.

He drew in a slow breath, then asked calmly, "Do you know where Mr. and Mrs. Smith are?"

Concern deepened the wrinkles on Mrs. Potts's face. She inched slowly closer and lowered her voice. "That's what has me so worried. Boyd was in the front yard when Angela yelled at him that Maggie had called and they had to get to the hospital right away. I hope nothing happened to that sweet child and her little boy, but Angela looked so upset."

The hospital? Maggie and Drew? A knot of hard, cold dread twisted Nick's stomach. Good God, had they gotten in an accident? Were they hurt? He'd seen too many accidents in his business, knew what could happen to bodies caught in buckled steel and smashed windows. Terror, like a living thing, slithered through his blood.

He couldn't remember saying goodbye to Mrs. Potts, couldn't even remember jumping on his motorcycle and starting the engine. The hospital in town wasn't far; he prayed that was the one they were at. There was another hospital in Ridgeville, about forty-five minutes from here, he thought, his mind racing through all the possibilities. She'd wanted to get away from him, so it was possible she'd driven to another town, to another airport where he couldn't find her.

Dammit, dammit. He forced every terrifying image from his mind, concentrated on simply getting to the hospital. When he roared into the parking lot, several people turned and stared, watched him as he ran into Emergency and cut in front of several people standing in line waiting for care.

"Maggie and Drew Smith, I mean Hamilton, Maggie

and Drew Hamilton,'' he yelled at the startled nurse behind the desk. "Were they checked in here?"

The nurse frowned at him, checked her paperwork, then shook her head. "If they came in an ambulance, I wouldn't have the paperwork yet. Go through the double doors into the back Emergency entrance."

He bolted through the doors and tore into the back Emergency rooms, but there was only one doctor and a nurse with a teenager having his knee stitched. No Maggie, no Drew.

A phone. He had to find a phone and call the next closest hospital. He'd find them, dammit, he'd find them if he had to call every damn hospital in a hundred-mile radius.

His hand was shaking when he found the phone in the central lobby waiting area and lifted the receiver. He was digging for a quarter in his jeans when he spotted a familiar figure half-hidden behind a newspaper.

Mr. Smith. He sat on the edge of a long, blue vinyl couch, reading the paper. Nick slowly replaced the phone receiver.

"Mr. Smith?"

Boyd Smith lowered his paper. He frowned darkly at Nick. "'Bout time you showed up."

"Maggie, Drew..." Nick could hardly get the words out. "Are they all right?"

"Of course they aren't all right," Boyd barked and tossed his paper aside.

The lump in Nick's throat swelled and moved into his chest. "How bad is it?"

"Bad enough," Boyd said tightly. "My Maggie, she's a tough little thing, she'll be all right. But Drew, he's just a boy. Kids don't always survive this sort of thing, and if they do, it leaves scars."

Don't always survive? Nick's knees gave out on him and he sank onto the couch beside Boyd. He couldn't accept this, that he might lose Drew after he'd just found him. He *wouldn't* accept it.

And what the hell did he care about scars? What did scars matter, as long as he lived?

Maggie. He needed to be with Maggie. God, how he needed her.

"Did you tell my daughter you were going to take my grandson away?"

Nick heard Boyd's question, but it took a moment to sink in. He closed his eyes on a long shuddering breath. Maggie's father had never spoken more than three words in a sentence, and now suddenly he was a regular yammer mouth. "I was angry, Mr. Smith. But this is hardly the time to discuss it."

"Seems like a good time to me. These things usually take a while. Least, that's how I seem to remember, even if it was twenty-nine years ago."

Great, Nick thought miserably. The man was not only babbling, he was babbling nonsense. "I'm not following you, Mr. Smith."

"Babies, Santos. Babies take a long time."

Babies? What in the world was he talking about? "Excuse me?"

Boyd frowned at him. "What's the matter with you? You're not the one having twins. What are you so pale for?"

Twins. Babies.

Babies.

A light flashed through the thick fog in his brain. *Julianna and Lucas.* They were having their babies. Today. Right now.

There was no accident. Maggie and Drew weren't hurt. They'd come to the hospital with Julianna.

Thank God, thank God, he repeated over and over, let his head fall into his hands as relief poured through him. When he started to laugh, Boyd leaned over and asked gruffly, "You okay, son?"

Nick felt weak and dizzy and so damn wonderful he almost grabbed Maggie's father and kissed him. Almost.

He stood quickly. "Where are they? Maggie and Drew?"

"Drew went with his grandmother to look for cookies in the cafeteria. Maggie was waiting with Julianna until Lucas got here, but he's been here a while now, so I'm not sure where she went to. Hey, you're not supposed to go—"

Nick pushed through the Keep Out doors and moved down the hallway. He had to find Maggie first, before he saw Drew. He heard the sound of a woman gasping for breath, then yelling at her husband, and hurriedly turned off the corridor. He had no intention of intruding on impending parenthood. He just had to find Maggie. If he waited one more minute, he thought he might explode. When an angry nurse hustled him out of the labor area and through another set of double doors, he started down another corridor.

When he came around the corner, he saw her. Standing in front of glass windows, staring inside. His heart pounded furiously as he moved closer. The nursery, he realized. She was looking at the babies.

His legs nearly folded at the sight of her. Exhaustion lined her pale brow, her shoulders were bowed, as if she carried the weight of the world there. She looked fragile, broken, like a delicate porcelain doll who'd fallen from her shelf.

He watched her, felt the emotions slam into him; the hurt, the anger. The love.

They had a child. The reality of that, the wonder, was just beginning to sink in. Drew was *his* son. He was a *father*. The thought truly staggered him, humbled him.

Maggie had lied, stolen something precious from him, but was it so impossible to understand why she'd done what she had? He tried to imagine what she'd felt after he'd made love to her and called her another woman's name, tried to imagine what she felt when that damn paternity suit was plastered all over the tabloids. Then he tried to imagine what he would have done. The truth was, he didn't know.

What he did know was that she accepted the responsibility, that she was a loving, caring mother and she'd sacrificed a great deal for her son.

For their son.

She turned, lifted her gaze to his. Panic flashed in her green eyes, then they went empty, cold, and she looked away.

"Maggie."

Hugging her arms tightly to her, she turned her back to him. He wanted to shake her; he wanted to kiss her. Instead, he shoved his hands into his pockets and moved beside her. They stood shoulder to shoulder, eyes straight ahead. Seconds, minutes passed. A lifetime, it seemed.

The hallway thundered with their silence.

"I was leaving," she said finally, and the weariness in her voice nearly had him reaching for her. "Taking Drew. I'd packed our bags and was on my way to the airport when I stopped to say goodbye to Julianna. I found her in the guest bedroom, where she'd been sewing when the labor pains hit hard. She was on the bed, doubled over. She'd tried to call Lucas, but his cell phone was busy. I got her in the car, managed to reach Lucas while we were on our way to the hospital.''

Nick swore softly. ''Lucas was with me. She must have tried to call when we were cleaning the grease out of his cell phone.''

Frowning, she glanced over her shoulder at him.

''It's a long story,'' he muttered. ''How is she now?''

Maggie turned her attention to the nursery again. ''They went into the delivery room about twenty minutes ago. She's a little early, but the doctor said the babies are strong and healthy and he wasn't expecting any problems.''

Nick closed his eyes on a sigh of relief. When he opened them again, he looked at the babies on the other side of the window and felt a sense of amazement fill him. One towheaded pink bundle was crying softly, one dark-haired blue bundle was wide-eyed. The other babies, two boys and a girl, were all sleeping peacefully. The sight was enough to make a grown man feel weak in the knees and soft in the gut.

''Did Drew look like that?'' Nick asked quietly.

Maggie's shoulders stiffened, then she nodded. ''Like that dark-haired baby on the right. His eyes were always wide open, looking, wanting to see everything.''

''Do you have pictures?''

When she turned, there were tears in her eyes. ''I have lots of pictures. And videos, too. I'll send them to you.''

He shook his head slowly. "It's not good enough."

"Nick," she said softly, her voice quavering, "I understand why you hate me. But I'm begging you, don't take Drew away from me."

"Drew is my son. He needs a father—" she started to back away from him, so he reached out and grabbed her shoulders "—and a mother."

She lifted her glistening gaze to his. "What are you saying? Joint custody?"

"Something like that." Those long, terrifying minutes he'd thought that Maggie and Drew had been hurt, that he might lose them forever, had tightly sealed the decision he'd already made before he'd even driven over to Maggie's house. "I want you to marry me."

"Marry you?" she whispered. "You'd marry me, even feeling the way you do about me, just for Drew?"

He laughed softly. "The way I feel about you is every reason to marry you. I love you, Maggie. I'm still mad as the devil, but you were bound to see my temper sooner or later. You'll have to learn to live with that, 'cause you're going to marry me, woman, and nothing, not the past, not the present, is going to stop that. I love you so much it's killing me, and if I'm not wrong, you love me, too."

Maggie went weak when Nick dragged her against him and covered her mouth with his—a deep, searing kiss that shot straight to her toes. The room began to spin, and she had to hold tightly to him for fear she would fall.

"You want me to marry you?" She touched his cheek, needed to know that this was real, that he was real, not part of the horrible nightmare she'd been living the past few hours. "Because you love me?"

He grinned at her. "There's probably a doctor

around here we can have check out your hearing if you need it, but first answer me, Maggie. Do you love me?''

She stared at him in astonishment. He didn't know? He really didn't know? She cupped his face in her hands, swallowed back the tears gathering in her throat. "We better get that same doctor to check your eyes, Nick Santos. If you can't see that I love you, that I've loved you since the day you saved me from Roger Gerckee, then you must be blind.''

His brow furrowed at Roger's name. "You mean at Lucas and Julianna's party?''

Laughing softly, she pressed her lips to his. "No, silly. In high school. The day Roger threw my lunch away and you dumped him in the trash can. I told you that you were my hero that day, but that was also the day I fell hopelessly in love with you.''

Amazement widened his eyes, then he narrowed them again. "And in North Carolina, the night we slept together? Were you in love with me, then?''

She nodded. "I was terrified of that assignment, knowing that I'd have to be close to you, talk to you. I knew I'd make an idiot out of myself." She closed her eyes and laid her head on his shoulder. "And I did. Because I loved you, I wanted you to be the first man I was with as much as I wanted to believe that you knew you were sleeping with me. When I realized the mistake I'd made, I couldn't face you again. Drew was the most wonderful, perfect gift, and though I was certain you'd want nothing to do with us, just having a part of you was more than I could ever have dreamed possible.''

He took her chin in his hand and lifted her face to his. "You're the damnedest woman," he said with a sigh. "We still need to fine tune a few facts, but we'll deal with that later. Right now I need you to do something for me."

His hand was shaking as he reached into his pocket and pulled out a ring. Maggie felt her breath catch as he slipped the diamond on her finger. "Marry me, Maggie. Stay with me here, in Wolf River, you and Drew. Please."

The diamond sparkled through the tears in her eyes. Her heart, the same heart that had shattered into thousands of pieces, swelled with the love she felt. "Yes." She whispered. "Yes, yes—"

He cut her off with his lips. She wrapped her arms around his neck, and poured all the love inside her into the kiss. He broke away suddenly, scooped her up in his arms and gave a shout. A nurse came around the corner, hands on her ample hips, and shushed them.

Laughing, he spun her, then set her down and grabbed her hand. "We've got someone to talk to, Maggie, darlin', and I don't plan on wasting one more minute."

"You move fast, Santos." Breathless, she let herself be pulled along. "Anybody ever tell you that?"

"All the time, darlin'." He stopped just long enough for a quick kiss, then hauled her down the corridor. "All the time."

Epilogue

Spring came early to Wolf River. The air was clear and clean. Tulips, red and yellow and pink, pushed through the sun-warmed soil in Lucas and Julianna's backyard. Purple pansies and white petunias wrestled for space in the beds, rose bushes heavy with buds promised a spectacular display in the next few weeks.

Just in time for the wedding, Maggie thought dreamily, letting her head rest on the back of Julianna's wicker chair while she stroked baby Nathaniel's down-soft hair. At four weeks, he had already outgrown his newborn clothes, unlike his sister, Nicole, who was nearly as dainty as the day she'd been born. They shared the same thick dark hair, but Nicole's skin was paler than Nathaniel's, her eyes blue to her brother's dark brown.

One boy, one girl, not two boys like Lucas and Julianna had thought. Maggie smiled, remembering the pleasure and pride on Lucas's face as he'd made the announcement at the hospital.

Julianna sat in the chair beside Maggie, gently rocking a sleeping Nicole in her arms. Babies and spring went together perfectly, Maggie decided. With the wedding set in two weeks, she calculated that if she got pregnant within the next two to three months, she and Nick would have their own spring baby.

And considering Nick's enthusiasm for the project, Maggie thought with a rush of heat, they would no doubt be successful. They'd have a girl this time, she thought with a smile. A little sister for Drew. She was certain of it.

The big wedding had been Nick's decision, though secretly she'd always dreamed of having one. When she'd married Richard, the ceremony had been simple, no nonsense, much like their marriage itself.

But nothing was simple with Nick. Everything was bigger than life and brightly colored, and their wedding would be no exception. The church. Family and friends. A garden reception here at the Blackhawks'. She still had to pinch herself that it was really happening, that she'd quit her job in New York, that a moving van was already on its way with her things from her apartment there.

That she was really marrying the man she'd loved more than half her life.

She glanced at the ring of her finger and smiled. Mrs. Nick Santos. The sound of it floated like music through her mind.

Another sound caught her attention: Drew's distant laughter. Her smile widened. It had been a little awkward trying to explain to Drew that Nick was his daddy, his *real* daddy, but children were more accepting, less interested in details than results. The only thing that mattered to him was that they were staying in Wolf River, that he had a new daddy he loved, and that they'd be moving into a house, a real house with a big yard he could play in and big trees he could climb. Between house hunting and wedding plans, the past four weeks had flown by, and she only hoped the next two would do the same.

Like native warriors returning from the hunt, they emerged from the woods, Drew and Nick and Lucas, proudly sporting their catch of silver trout on a string.

"Mom, look what Daddy and I caught in the creek," Drew yelled excitedly. "Uncle Lucas says we're gonna clean 'em out here, so we don't make you and Aunt Julianna sick at the sight of blood and guts."

"How considerate of Uncle Lucas." Julianna shifted a softly whimpering Nicole in her arms, then grinned at Maggie. "Looks like you're all staying for a fish fry."

Maggie grinned back. Julianna and Lucas had accepted her and Drew from the beginning, brought them into their family without question, without judgment of the past. Maggie felt that she'd not only found a friend in Julianna, but a sister, as well.

The front doorbell sounded and Julianna groaned. "It's Mrs. Waters from the Women's League. She was going to pick up a quilt I made for the bazaar next week, but the woman could talk the ears off a beagle. After that night I had with these two darlin's, I'm just not in the mood."

When Julianna started to get up, Maggie waved her back down. "Let me talk to her. If you're going to feed my men, it's the least I can do. If I'm not back in an hour, though, send out the rescue party."

"Bless you." Julianna rocked an increasingly fussy Nicole. "The quilt's on the dining room table."

Maggie was cooing softly against Nathaniel's soft temple when she opened the front door. But it wasn't Mrs. Waters standing on the doorstep. Not even close.

Killian Shawnessy.

Eyes wide, all Maggie could do was stare at him. She hadn't seen him in at least ten years, but it was Ian, all right. His dark hair was shorter, his shoulders wider and chest broader, his handsome, angled face tanned. He wore aviator sunglasses, but she could see the fine lines at the corners of his eyes when he smiled slowly.

"Ian," she breathed his name on an exhale.

"Well, if it isn't little Margaret Smith," he drawled. "Nick told me you'd changed, but he didn't quite capture the magnitude of that understatement."

Maggie blushed, then leaned to the side and looked behind Ian. He glanced over his shoulder and raised his brows. "Looking for someone?"

"Only the trail of swooning women."

He grinned at her, then nodded at the baby. "I know Nick works fast, but I don't think even he can speed that process up. I take it this is Lucas and Julianna's?"

She nodded. "This is Nathaniel. Why don't you come in and meet his sister?"

He followed her to the back porch, where Julianna stared at him with the same wide-eyed astonishment.

When she was finally able to catch her breath, Julianna jumped up and gave him a hug. "Ian Shawnessy! Is that really you? When in the world did you get here?"

Maggie could have sworn that the sudden rosy color

on Ian's cheeks was a blush, but when he glanced down at the baby in Julianna's arms, his face seemed to pale.

"Uh, a little while ago." He stepped back, kept his eyes on the baby as if it might attack. "I'm renting a cabin up on the river."

"Maggie and I have to go tell Lucas and Nick." There was a wicked light in Julianna's eyes as she looked at Maggie, then at her daughter who'd started to cry. "Here, Nicole, sweetie, say hello to your Uncle Ian. Mommy will be right back."

Before he could protest, Julianna thrust her daughter into Ian's big arms. Eyes wide, he opened his mouth, but couldn't quite get the words out. Maggie winked at Julianna, then followed suit by placing Nathaniel into Ian's other arm. He turned white, and the look in his eyes was sheer terror.

"Hey…wait…come back…." He sounded as if he were choking.

"You are an evil woman, Julianna," Maggie said, laughing as they ran to get Lucas and Nick.

"I'm paying him back for not showing up at our wedding." She glanced over her shoulder and giggled. "Imagine a big, grown man terrified of a couple of little babies."

"Think there's any hope for him?"

"There's always hope." She grinned. "Look at Lucas and Nick."

"Look at us what?" Lucas came up from the side of the creek, a bucket of fish in his hand. Nick, with Drew on his heels, was right behind.

"We have company, boys. The last of the bad boys has returned."

Nick and Lucas looked at each other in bewilderment, then slowly grinned. "Shawnessy," they said together.

"In the flesh." Julianna looked toward the back porch. She could hear both babies crying now. "But you better hurry. He might pass out while he's holding our son and daughter."

A strangled cry for help drifted from the house. With a whoop, Lucas headed for the house, Julianna right behind him. Nick started to follow, then stopped, scooped up Maggie in one arm and Drew in the other. He swung them around until Maggie was breathless and Drew dizzy with laughter.

The intensity in his gaze as his mouth caught hers, and the fierce, possessive kiss brought a burning moisture to her eyes.

"Damn, it's good to be home," he murmured against her lips.

Maggie smiled as they walked back to the house. She couldn't have agreed with him more.

* * * * *

Mystery man Killian is back! Don't miss his story, KILLIAN'S PASSION, available next month from Silhouette Desire.

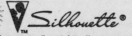

If you enjoyed what you just read,
then we've got an offer you can't resist!

Take 2 bestselling
love stories FREE!
Plus get a FREE surprise gift!

 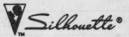

SILHOUETTE® Desire®

Get ready to enter the exclusive, masculine world of the...

TEXAS Cattleman's Club

Silhouette Desire®'s powerful new miniseries features five wealthy Texas bachelors—all members of the state's most prestigious club—who set out on a mission to rescue a princess...and find true love!

TEXAS MILLIONAIRE—August 1999
by Dixie Browning (SD #1232)
CINDERELLA'S TYCOON—September 1999
by Caroline Cross (SD #1238)
BILLIONAIRE BRIDEGROOM—October 1999
by Peggy Moreland (SD #1244)
SECRET AGENT DAD—November 1999
by Metsy Hingle (SD #1250)
LONE STAR PRINCE—December 1999
by Cindy Gerard (SD #1256)

Available at your favorite retail outlet.

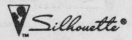

Silhouette®